## Kyle was right to sound skeptical

"Suddenly remembered Rhys? He's repairing the fence down there." Kyle moved behind Arminel, positioned her face and pointed.

The next moment she was enfolded in his arms and Kyle's mouth was moving with practiced seduction over hers. She was unable to resist his intimate intense exploration.

Quite suddenly she knew he was beyond control—if she could not stop him, he, a perfect stranger, would be master of her body. She concentrated on fighting, not him but herself, until he dropped his arms.

"You wanted me as much as I wanted you, Arminel."

"I know—I must have been mad."

"Try and convince yourself." Kyle had recovered more quickly than Arminel. "Shall I tell Rhys that you respond equally fervently to any man who kisses you?"

# Books by Robyn Donald

## HARLEQUIN PRESENTS

## HARLEQUIN ROMANCES

These books may be available at your local bookseller.

For a free catalog listing all titles currently available,
send your name and address to:

Harlequin Reader Service
P.O. Box 52040, Phoenix, AZ 85072-2040
Canadian address: Stratford, Ontario N5A 6W2

# ROBYN DONALD

## a durable fire

**Harlequin Books**

TORONTO • NEW YORK • LONDON
AMSTERDAM • PARIS • SYDNEY • HAMBURG
STOCKHOLM • ATHENS • TOKYO • MILAN

For
MEGAN

Harlequin Presents first edition June 1984
ISBN 0-373-10696-3

Original hardcover edition published in 1984
by Mills & Boon Limited

Printed in U.S.A.

# CHAPTER ONE

AT the doors that led into the departure hall he asked with cold composure, 'Have you your passport ready?'

Beneath her breath she said, 'Yes, it's in my bag. I checked it a moment ago.'

All around them was the last-minute bustle of the airport, people kissing goodbye, children already waving, a few tears, barely suppressed excitement. Arminel Lovett cast a desperate glance around, her dark blue eyes stretched so wide that she bore the same glazed stare as a doll. Her rare, luminous beauty drew stares, some surreptitious, some open. Beside her, her tall escort was impossibly remote, his hard handsome face bored until he caught the eye of a man who was staring openly; then the light grey eyes flashed a warning fierce enough to abash the brash onlooker.

In spite of having her attention fixed with painful intensity on him Arminel missed this piece of byplay. She dared not look at him, for she knew the exact degree of contempt in his glance whenever it rested on her, but she could feel his nearness with every cell in her body. It took all the willpower that she possessed not to break down, but somehow she managed to project a kind of detached aloofness to hide the anguish which twisted her heart.

'Kyle,' she began, her voice catching on his name. 'Kyle, can't we——?'

Very curtly he interrupted. 'There's nothing more to say——'

And was interrupted in his turn by the cultured impersonal voice over the loudspeaker. 'Would passengers for Air New Zealand flight B134 to Brisbane please make their way to the departure hall. This is the last call . . .'

Kyle Beringer looked down at the girl beside him. 'Goodbye,' he said, finality hardening the already cold tones to ice.

She lifted her smooth black head proudly, met his gaze with one of equal composure. 'Goodbye, Kyle. It was an education meeting you,' she said, irony sharpening her voice before she walked without a backward glance through the doors, her slender body rigid, head held high above shoulders firmly straight.

For a moment he stood watching her, his expression darkening, then he turned and with the smooth stride of an athlete made his way to the exit, ignoring the many frankly speculative and appreciative glances which came his way from the feminine half of the crowd.

Somehow Arminel managed to retain her command of herself throughout the departure formalities, smiling as she made a noncommittal reply to the Customs Officer who asked her if she had enjoyed her holiday in New Zealand, waiting quietly in the lounge until they were marshalled on to the DC10. First class, of course; Kyle had booked her seat. It probably hadn't occurred to him that she had ever travelled on anything other than first class. Certainly no Beringer ever did.

Once on board she sat quietly, head averted as the hostess went through the emergency drill. There were not very many passengers in this part of the big jet, and those who were there settled down with the poise of experienced travellers, blasé about the three-and-a-half-hour flight in front of them. It was raining lightly; the late spring day had been warm and tempting as they drove out, but now it had clouded over. Arminel did not even glance out as the plane taxied smoothly off on to the runway.

But when the engines picked up speed she turned her face away from the light and impersonal cheerfulness of the interior and let the pent-up tears slide from her eyes.

Just for a few minutes, she promised herself, but tension too long repressed becomes uncontrollable, and ten minutes later she was still weeping, silently yet with a desperation which finally alerted one of the stewardesses.

'Can I get you something?' she asked as she bent over Arminel, shielding her from the gaze of anyone who might be curious.

'No, thank you.' Arminel managed to stem the flow for long enough to make it look as though she was over the worst.

'Well, ring, won't you, if you'd like a drink. Sometimes it's the only thing that helps.' And with this wry wisdom the woman went on her way.

Groping in her bag for another tissue, Arminel found to her horror that the tears would not be denied. Fiercely she wiped her eyes and cheeks, willing herself to be more sensible, to stop this embarrassing weakness before she made a complete laughing stock of herself. And still the tears oozed from beneath her lashes as though possessed of a will of their own. Her only consolation was that there was no one near enough to see her undignified anguish.

It came as a shock, therefore, when a masculine voice said, as someone slid into the seat beside her, 'She was right, you know. What you need is a stiff drink. You're suffering from shock.'

Choking, unable to summon up the usual freezing courtesy with which she normally repelled unwelcome advances, Arminel shook her head, wishing despairingly that people would just leave her alone so that she could find release from her grief in her own way.

'You're upsetting the stewardess,' the voice went on inexorably, 'and me, too.'

'Please, I can't ... I'm not ...' She had to blow her nose because her voice was thick and indistinct, and then more tears began to chase themselves down the exquisite curve of her cheek.

'No, you're not, are you?' Whoever he was he was quite accustomed to dealing with weeping women. Like Kyle.

He said something she didn't catch and a minute later a glass was put into her reluctant hand. 'Drink it down. All of it,' he said.

It was an order, one Arminel was too limp to disobey. She spluttered as the liquid burnt a track down her throat and shook her head.

'All of it,' he repeated inexorably.

Obediently she sipped at the stuff, too exhausted to feel anything more than this meek submission. And they had been right, he and the stewardess, for the brandy brought a cautious glow to her body, stilling the humiliating tears. Arminel stared straight ahead while she drank it, refusing to look at her rescuer, but she was very conscious of him. A swift sideways glance revealed hands which were lean and well-shaped resting on long, expensively-clad legs.

When she had finished the drink he ordered another, saying calmly, 'Take this a little slower. And sometimes it helps to talk to someone you're never likely to meet again.'

This time she turned her head to look at him, her eyes dark with rejection. About forty, or a little younger, he was good-looking in a conventional way, with regular features. The only claims to distinction were a jaw which promised determination and eyes of a considerable shrewdness, eyes which at the moment bore the arrested expression to which she was accustomed. It was the usual masculine tribute to the accident of heredity which had given her the face and body of an enchantress.

Slowly, as if the words were torn from him, he said, 'How incredibly lovely you are.'

Fiercely, leaving him in no doubt as to her sincerity, she choked, 'I wish to God I was as ugly as sin!'

Instantly the stunned expression was replaced by comprehension. 'You must forgive me. I'm not usually so inept. If you'd like to tell me about it I'll not annoy you with any more insensitive compliments.'

When she hesitated, he continued softly, 'I'm not trying to pick you up. I think you need to talk to someone and I assure you that I'm quite trustworthy. And like most men, I hate to see a woman cry. In any case, you're almost young enough to be my daughter.'

'I'm old enough to cause a pack of trouble,' she said drearily, no longer resisting the insidious temptation to ease her pain by confiding in this pleasant stranger. It could do no harm. As he had said, they were most unlikely to meet after this flight, and something in his face and manner inspired confidence and trust. Her long slender fingers turned the glass as she looked down into it, her voice level, almost monotonous when she spoke.

'I should have chosen almost any other place but the entrance to the shopping complex by the beach at Surfers Paradise. . . .'

But Karen was new to Surfers and she wasn't too sure that she could find her way to any of the other places Arminel had suggested over the telephone. So they had arranged a time, and, of course, Karen was late. She wouldn't be Karen if she hadn't been. Arminel waited, watching the crowds of holidaymakers in their light summery clothes even though this was the depths of winter. At Surfers it didn't matter; the nights were cool, but during the day the sun shone benignly down on to the glorious beach and the busy, pleasant town beside it. Karen was taking a bus tour from Sydney to the beautiful tropical shores of Northern Queensland and had a day to spend in Surfers on the way. It was the first time they had met for over a year since Arminel had left a boring job in Sydney to come up here.

Her eyes roamed the holiday crowd, searching rather anxiously for Karen's small, curvy figure. Arminel enjoyed life here; all but one aspect of it. And, sure enough, before long a man tried to pick her up. She had been conscious of his stare for some minutes, but even her haughty aloofness hadn't intimidated him. He was old enough to know better, a good-looking beach boy who probably preyed on lonely women on holiday, and he would not leave her alone.

'Listen, push off!' she was finally goaded into saying, anger colouring skin like warm satin.

He laughed knowingly. 'Boy, you look even prettier when you're mad! Come on, don't be stuck-up. I can give you a good time, better than whoever you're waiting for.'

'Oh, get lost!' And when he just smiled she spat, 'If you don't leave me alone, I'll——'

He leered, 'You'll what? Those pretty hands couldn't hurt a fly. Anyway. I like it when a girl plays rough.'

She was really exasperated now, and was just about to tell him exactly what she thought of him when a voice from behind made both of them turn.

'You heard what the lady said,' it drawled. 'How about moving on now, boy?'

Or it will give me great pleasure to assist you on your way, the stranger intimated without any need for words. About three inches taller than the pest, her rescuer was built like a rugby forward, all muscle and strength and self-confidence.

Well, that had been the end of the pest. By the time Karen finally arrived her rescuer had introduced himself as Rhys Beringer, on holiday from New Zealand, had discovered her name and was proceeding to make the most of the situation.

It was no wonder Karen couldn't hide her astonishment. Bitter experience, beginning at a tender age, had made Arminel so wary that, as Karen had often teased her, she wasn't interested in any man unless he came with references and certificated to prove that he was harmless.

'But Rhys is different,' Arminel said, astounded herself at her quick acceptance of the man.

'Better looking than most,' Karen mocked, stirring her coffee and basking in the reflected glory of being with the most beautiful girl in the restaurant. 'And he has that very, very upper crust accent. Money, too, I'll bet. Those clothes didn't cost anything less than a small fortune, and he wore them as casually as if he was well used to them. When are you meeting him again?'

'Tomorrow, at lunchtime.' Arminel blushed. 'O.K., so it's not like me, but he really is different, Karo.'

'For your sake I hope so.' Karen often assumed a mask of cynicism, but this time she was fervent. 'You've had rather bad luck with your men, haven't you?'

'The nice ones are frightened of this stupid face,' Arminel said wearily, 'and the others seem to see me as a face and a body, nothing else.'

Karen smiled. 'I used to wish that I was a raving beauty, but I'm rather glad that I'm not. It doesn't seem to make for happiness. Why don't you exploit it? Go modelling, or something like that.'

'I've thought about it, but I enjoy what I'm doing. I know life in a lawyer's office doesn't sound like any young girl's dream, but it's interesting, and I'm good at it. I like it.'

'Yes, it seems a pity you've got brains as well,' Karen murmured. 'You'd probably find things easier if you didn't think so much.'

In the light of what followed this was ironically amusing, for Rhys Beringer insisted on meeting her at lunchtime and every night, and made her laugh and teased her and treated her with the kind of gallantry which soon persuaded her into relaxing her guard. Not all at once, for she hadn't really trusted a man since that first frightening experience when she was sixteen, but before his three weeks' holiday was up she knew that she was going to miss him unbearably when he went back.

'Why don't you come over?' he suggested the night before he was due to leave. When she hesitated, torn between a singing delight and the knowledge that holiday romances rarely grew into anything more permanent, he urged, 'It's time you saw a little bit of the world, and there's no one but yourself to think about. I know you have no relations here.'

'As far as I know, none anywhere,' she said. Her parents had been English immigrants, and when her mother ran away with another man her father had been forced to put her into care. After a while he, too, had drifted away, leaving her to all intents and purposes an orphan. Not that it had been too bad. She had been happy enough in the large house with pleasant foster-parents and a big 'family' of other children in similar situations. She still kept in touch with several of them; Karen was one. But those early rejections, and the effect of her physical beauty on men, had forced her to strengthen the skin she had grown over her emotions, the skin which Rhys had penetrated so easily.

Now she stirred in his arms, her body suffused with the warm sweetness his kisses caused. 'Oh, Rhys, this has been a fairy story,' she said huskily. 'It wouldn't be the same in the cold light of day.'

'Not for you, perhaps, but I know how I feel,' he said stubbornly. 'I'm sure that if you let yourself you'll feel the same way.' His voice deepened persuasively as he whispered in her ear, 'Give it a try, Arminel. It's not as though it's on the other side of the world. It's only twelve hundred miles across the Tasman Sea.'

She was tempted, oh, how she was tempted, but as well as twelve hundred miles of sea there was also the matter of plane tickets, although she had enough money saved to pay for those, and if it didn't work out she could always call it a holiday. And that was the rub, for it wouldn't be a holiday; she had just had one, so she would have to resign from her good, well-paid job, and with the economic situation the way it was, positions like that were no longer as easy to find as they had been.

'Of course you'd stay at Te Nawe,' he coaxed, kissing her ear.

'Te Nawe? What's that?'

He laughed as her tongue tripped over the unfamiliar syllables. 'It's where I live. It's a station in the north of New Zealand, not too far from the sea, not too far from a town and not too far from the mountains. You'll like it.'

'I'm sure I would,' she returned drily, pulling away as the familiar desolation washed over her. 'You know I can't do that, Rhys. It might not matter in New Zealand, but that sort of behaviour gets you talked about here.'

He grinned down at her, his hand clasping hers. 'Idiot! I have a perfectly good mother tucked away there, as well as a big brother. Think you'd be safe enough?'

Sudden laughter bubbled up in her throat, laughter sweetened by relief and a burgeoning hope that at last she might have met a man who could see beyond the deceptive allure of her physical attributes. 'I like the sound of the mother,' she said gaily, 'but I'm not too sure about the brother.'

'Just keep it like that,' he said meaningly. 'I'm very fond of Kyle, but he does tend to have a devastating effect on women, even mine, who should know better.'

'*He* does,' she teased, squeezing his fingers. 'What about you?'

'Oh, I'm in a very minor league compared to Kyle.' He sounded rueful and perfectly serious. 'You know the sort of thing. Dad died when we were kids and as Kyle is the oldest he's had to take on the responsibility, and there's plenty of that. As well as Te-Nawe there are other stations, and an assortment of related businesses. Kyle is big enough to cope, but too much too soon made him a hard man. There's no way I could measure up to Kyle, and normally I'm happy enough to have it like that. I get the fun and he gets the kudos.'

Arminel moved a little closer to him. 'He sounds rather forbidding.'

'I suppose he is.' He tugged gently at her hand, urging her along the beach. It was late, but there was the light of a large moon to show them the way. They had dined well, drunk champagne, and now neither of them wanted to end the evening, even though Rhys left early the next morning.

Some yards down the yielding sand he resumed, 'Oh, he's forbidding, and tough as granite, but I'd be lying if I didn't tell you that women tend to lose their heads over him. It's that air of leashed power, I suppose. One look at Kyle and you know that there's nothing in this world that he can't cope with. That's what women like, isn't it? Security?'

'I think that most of us want love,' she said softly. 'That's the greatest security.'

Rhys hugged her suddenly. 'You're nice,' he said thickly. 'Nice, like an apple, sweet and clean and crisp. Arminel, I've fallen headlong in love with you. When you come to Te Nawe come as my love, wearing my ring?'

Her heart blocked her throat. She lifted her eyes, met his pleading gaze with a luminous, trembling smile, and knew that she could not accept his proposal. 'It wouldn't be fair,' she said. 'Your mother has the right to be told about me before you decide anything. And you could change your mind before I get there.' It was an effort to keep her voice light, almost playful. 'It does happen, you know.'

'It won't to me,' he promised definitely, bending his head to her mouth, his kisses filled with the same pleading she had seen in his eyes.

It was hard to stand firm, especially when he showed her the ring he had chosen for her, a sapphire as dark as her eyes enfolded in diamonds, but she knew that she could not suddenly turn up at his home as his fiancée. They had only known each other for three weeks; it just wasn't long enough.

'Oh, sweetheart, I love you so,' he whispered, pressing a kiss into the palm of each of her hands.

'Make your arrangements as soon as you can, please. I'll be waiting for you.'

But he wasn't. A month later when she arrived at the airport in Auckland it was to find herself without anyone to meet her. After a few bewildered moments she carried her suitcase to a seat and sat down. The flight had been bumpy and she was tired, still worried about her reception at Te Nawe, which she now knew from Rhys's letters to be several hours' journey north of Auckland. Possibly Rhys had been delayed. Perhaps he was unable to get to a phone to let her know.

The passengers on her plane dissipated, were replaced by those from a Singapore jet, and then she heard her name over the loudspeaker, asking her to report to the Air New Zealand counter.

And sure enough, there he was, dazzling the receptionist if the bemused look on the girl's face was anything to go by. He had his back to Arminel, but she would have recognised him anywhere.

'Rhys?' she said, half a pace away. And he turned, and it wasn't Rhys.

Her half-excited, half-worried smile fled. Her outstretched hand was ignored as Kyle Beringer looked her over, very thoroughly, with eyes of the clearest, coldest grey she had ever seen, cloud-grey, ice-grey, eyes that surveyed her with a total lack of emotion. Chilled into a quick withdrawal, her expression tightened against the implacable frost of his gaze.

'Miss Lovett?'

His voice was deeper than Rhys's, deeper and crisper and far harder.

Her tongue came out to dampen her lip before she could speak. Not only her lips were dry; somehow his presence made both her mouth and her throat feel parched.

She felt as though she was choking over stale bread as she replied. 'Yes, I'm Arminel Lovett. You must be Rhys's brother.'

'Kyle Beringer.' An imperative hand was stretched forward. Numbly she gave him her suitcase, watched as he turned to say something charming to the extremely interested receptionist, and allowed herself to be shepherded out through the sliding glass doors.

The wind cut through her jeans and light woollen top with the savagery of a buzz-saw. Shivering, scurrying along to keep up with him, she pulled on the jacket she had taken care to carry, well aware that Auckland was considerably farther away from the Equator than Queensland.

His long legs didn't check stride to accommodate her. When they arrived at the car, a big, opulent thing in dark green, mud-splattered yet obviously well cared for, he unlocked the boot to put her case in, then came around and unlocked the door on the passenger's side in the front, giving her no chance as to where she sat.

Inside the luxurious vehicle it was warm. Arminel's teeth clamped a moment on to her bottom lip as he walked around the bonnet. Lord, but he was big! Broad shoulders which not even the subdued business suit could disguise, long legs which must put him a couple of inches higher than Rhys who was just six feet, and an aura of total, well-founded self-assurance. Power personified, he moved with lithe grace, not the lumbering gait of so many big men.

Against the turbulent grey sky his profile was incisive, beautiful with the cold strength of perfect bone structure. Manlike, Rhys hadn't thought to mention that his brother had the countenance of a dark angel. For a moment fear paled Arminel's skin, made her shiver with a clammy foresight. Then it was replaced by determination. She was not Kyle Beringer's affair. She and Rhys were the ones who had to decide.

But at least she was forewarned. If Mrs Beringer was as formidable as the man who met her she was going to have to tread warily.

When he swung himself into the driver's seat she was pulling off her coat.

'Here,' he said impatiently, holding out a hand.

'It's all right, I'll keep it on my knee.'

'And simmer quietly? It can go in the back.'

Because it was a small, stupid thing to fuss over she handed it to him; their fingers touched and she could not stop her swift jerk back as though the small contact stung.

For a split second those strange, pale eyes pierced hers before he turned and deposited the coat on to the back seat.

Then he stripped off his jacket, revealing the lean breadth of his shoulders. As his jacket joined hers on the back seat Arminel swallowed, averting her eyes. Beneath the white shirt muscles moved; she felt an odd drowning sensation and fixed her eyes on to her hands, forcing herself to acknowledge the pale pink nail polish, the small silver ring which was her only legacy from her mother.

He said nothing, but she was shaken and twitchy, only too acutely aware of the silent blast of antagonism emanating from him. The air in the car seemed to be full of wires, bristling with tension that bewildered and angered her. What on earth had caused it?

For it was not just coming from him. Beneath the thin wool of her jersey her heart beat loudly, faster than normal, and the palms of her hands were damp. Odd sensations were racing through her taut body, sensitising every inch of her skin so that she felt that she was on fire. Love at first sight was a well-known institution, although not one in which she believed, but this must be its direct opposite, instantaneous dislike. She had been prepared to like him, but that first hard survey had banished that; she felt it would take very little for her to learn to hate him.

As he did her. But surely hate was the wrong word? His expression had given little away, but she was certain that there had been a moment of shock before the icy surge of contempt which had so quickly erected her defences.

They had been driving for ten minutes or so before she tired of the silence. Swallowing, for her throat seemed blocked, she asked, 'Where is Rhys? When he wrote he said he'd be meeting the plane.'

To her surprise—and pleasure—her voice sounded quite calm and composed.

Kyle Beringer said coldly, 'He's at Te Nawe, working. In spite of—everything—we do work, Miss Lovett.'

'I'm sure you do.' A hint of fire warmed the intense blue of her gaze. In a clipped voice she continued, 'I hope my arrival hasn't put you out, Mr Beringer.'

'Not at all. I was already in Auckland.'

And that apparently was that. He could not have made his disapproval of her any more obvious if he'd hired a plane to emblazon it across the sky. Arminel turned her head to stare unseeingly out of the window. Such open antagonism upset her, but it also brought into being an unshakeable determination which was so much at variance with her fragile, seductive beauty that its presence usually astonished those who came into contact with it. Delicately her chin lifted; the fine profile hardened. If Kyle Beringer wanted a fight, she was perfectly prepared to give him one for his money. Or rather for his brother. She might look a frail thing, but hidden beneath that slender exterior there was resolution and will-power and courage.

Rhys had said that Kyle was attractive to women. Here was one who found him thoroughly repelling, she thought grimly.

There was a lot of Auckland. Some of it was pretty; it was certainly green in spite of the houses, green with a vividness which the intermittent rain only intensified. The motorway swept through the suburbs, revealing flowering trees and neat, green lawns. A wilderness of concrete intimidated as they drove through interchanges in the backyard of the city before swooping over a bridge that crossed an arm of the harbour.

In spite of the prickly atmosphere inside the car Arminel was interested in the landscape, finding the tiny humps of the volcanoes especially intriguing. There seemed so many of them! Grass covered their steep terraced sides except for the much bigger one out in the harbour, which was dark purple with trees.

Unable to contain her curiosity, she asked, 'What are the lines around the volcanoes? Sheep tracks?'

'They were used as forts by the Maori people,' he told her. 'The terraces are the remnants of the fortifications they needed to keep each other at bay. They were brilliant tacticians who dug trenches and used rows of sharpened stakes as protection.'

She nodded. 'If this is volcanic then the soil must be rich.'

'Very. This area was known as Tamaki-makau-rau, Tamaki of a thousand lovers, because it was a contested land. Tamaki means battle. The old Maoris were a proud, vigorous, warlike race.'

'How old are the volcanoes?' At the swift sardonic glance she shrugged. 'Well, give or take a million years. They look so little and new, like a child's efforts at landscaping. Like sand castles.'

'In geographical terms they're young, less than a hundred thousand years old. Rangitoto,' with a nod at the island she had noticed from the bridge, 'is only a few hundred years old. If you look out to the left you'll see an almost circular bay behind the road. There's another farther on. They're the remnants of other eruptions—as are the hills on the horizon behind us, the Waitakeres.'

'Life must have been pretty lively around here for a while.'

'Fortunately there were no people here,' he said on a note of condescension which immediately set her hackles up.

Without pondering the wisdom of such a course she replied tartly, 'I know. The Maori people came here about a thousand years ago, didn't they?'

'Yes. They sailed from Tahiti, probably by way of the Cook Islands. Carbon dating at archaeological sites shows that they were here by 900 A.D.' There was a pause, then he added, 'Been checking up, Miss Lovett?'

As a child it had been her dream to become an archaeologist. Circumstances had prevented that, but she had always retained an interest in the subject. And if one lived on the fringes of the vast Pacific Ocean as she had all her life then an interest in archaeology meant an interest in the Polynesians, of whom the Maori people were a branch. Setting out in their double-hulled canoes, they had criss-crossed the wide waters from Hawaii to Easter Island to New Zealand, colonising as they went; South Seas Vikings, as one of their famous descendants had called them. She had read Sir Peter Buck's book, *Vikings of the Sunrise*, and thrilled to the tale of these noble, barbaric people.

But she did not like the insinuation in Kyle's deep voice or the undertone of contempt that accompanied it. With a brusqueness which was a startling contrast to her appearance she retorted, 'Of course. I always feel that to get the best out of a holiday one should learn as much as possible about the place one wants to go to.'

'And this is—a holiday?' The cold grey eyes lanced her way again, leaving her with every muscle tensed for flight.

'Somehow,' he continued, 'I think Rhys is sure that he'll be able to persuade you to stay.'

And you, she thought warily, are just as determined to see that I go. But why? What was it that had set him so against her?

This superb, expensive car provided one reason. She had known that Rhys's family were wealthy, but this was the sort of vehicle owned only by those who had no need at all to watch their expenditure. So the Beringers were not just wealthy; they were, to coin a phrase, stinking rich. Did he think she was some cheap little fortune-hunter on the make for a rich husband?

Her hands clenched on to themselves. Unwilling she glanced across at the cutting line of his profile. Yes, he would think that. There was no softness in his features beyond a hint of sensuality in the beautifully moulded mouth. Kyle Beringer was not the sort of man who fell in love, or even believed in it. No doubt his marriage would be contracted for practical reasons, the desire for children, his need for a hostess and a permanent lover to keep him satisfied when he was tired of playing the field.

Anger flicked a small muscle beside her mouth, tightened the soft line of her lips. She had never disliked a man as much as she did this one, and she had a horrible foreboding that he roused the sort of emotions that did not dissipate with better knowledge. It had been the same for him, too; she had felt the whip of his glance in that first moment of seeing her, and although he had obviously been prepared to dislike her there could be no doubt that his reaction was stronger, more basic than his objection to a possibly money-hungry girl-friend of his brother allowed.

Her first instinct was to tell him bluntly that as far as she was concerned this was a holiday, a time when she and Rhys would discover what their true feelings for each other were. But a kind of loyalty kept her silent. Rhys, obviously angered by his brother's attitude, must have said more than he should, and she could not now make him look a fool by refuting it.

Mixed with that loyalty was anger at the cold arrogance of the man beside her. He would be the one who looked a fool when the decisions were made, whatever they were. If that lovely warmth she had felt with Rhys was love then Kyle would look stupid for assuming her to be on the catch, but if their attraction faded and died in the cold light of reality, then she would demand an apology before she left. She probably wouldn't get one. Kyle Beringer was the kind of autocrat who walked the earth totally confident of his own authority.

Perhaps she should have asked herself why she felt so strongly about the man; even how she knew so much about him. She might have convinced herself that it was no more than the intuition all women felt when threatened, long generations of servitude and submission sharpening every sense so that the war of the sexes was fought on a little more equal basis.

But she didn't wonder then at the strength of her reaction to him. Not then.

# CHAPTER TWO

THE road wound its way around hills and along narrow river valleys, for the first hour or so not too far from the sea. Then there was a landscape of quite steep hills, almost all grassed except for a few which were covered in sombre pines, and others with the olive-green native bush hiding their contours. The road was excellent, skilful engineering minimising the sharp rises and abrupt falls, until they left the main route and headed roughly east along a narrow gravel road. After a few miles this deteriorated into a stretch of potholes and corrugations. The big car made light of them, but Arminel shuddered at the thought of travelling along it in a smaller car with less luxurious springing.

Here the hills pressed aganst the road, their high grassy contours tufted with clumps of trees and scrub. A small stream ran down beside them, its banks ridged with strange spiky bushes which she recognised as New Zealand flax, and some kind of tree which resembled a smaller flax-bush on a palm trunk.

Again curiosity unlocked her lips.

'Cabbage trees,' Kyle Beringer told her. 'I believe they're most closely related to a lily. The Maoris and the early settlers used to eat the heart leaves as a vegetable, hence the name. They grow near water and in swampy ground.'

She nodded, unable to overcome her anger at the curt lack of interest in his tones. 'How much farther is Te Nawe?'

'Only a few kilometres. We're half an hour from the nearest town. A far cry from Surfers, I'm afraid.'

'Yes.' She would *not* be provoked into an unwise reply. 'What does Te Nawe mean?'

'The Scar.' A brief pause before he went on, 'I'm surprised that Rhys didn't tell you. He seems to have been remarkably free with other information.'

'Perhaps he didn't think I'd be interested,' she countered with sweet malice. 'Mind you, we were rather too absorbed in each other to be paying much attention to anything else. Why is it called The Scar? It's an unusual name.'

If her reply angered him he gave no sign of it, the cold imperturbable voice smooth and bland as he said, 'Te Nawe hill is marred by an enormous landslip which must have happened some hundreds of years ago. It's almost re-covered by vegetation now, but at the time it was named it stood out like a scar. It was used as a beacon by ships. Most of the trade and travelling was by sea in those days.'

'Can you see the sea from the farm?'

'Yes, from almost all of it. We're only half a mile from the coast.'

Well, Rhys had said it was close enough to the sea. Certainly close enough to the mountains, she thought, looking straight over the edge of the road which here wound its way around an almost sheer drop to a valley some hundreds of feet below.

'Do you drive, Miss Lovett?' he asked.

'No.'

'A pity,' he observed. 'You'll be shut away here. Perhaps you should get Rhys to teach you—if you're here long enough.'

What she would have replied was lost as an enormous silver tanker truck met them on the corner. There wasn't room—she drew in a sharp, terrified breath, her hands clenching on her knees as the two vehicles passed each other with surely only inches to spare.

Not that either driver seemed at all concerned. Indeed, as soon as he saw them the tanker driver had given a short toot on his horn, a toot answered by

Kyle's wave. Putting them at risk by taking his hand from the wheel!

'I don't think so,' she said weakly on an expelled breath. 'Not if it means that I could be meeting juggernauts like that around any corner. What on earth was it?'

'A milk tanker. The milk is collected from the dairy farms every day and taken to the factory, where it's made into cheese and milk powder.' He slid a sideways glance at her face, noting the colour only slowly coming back into the golden skin. Against the fragile temple tendrils of fine black hair clung, damp with the sudden perspiration the truck had caused.

'Then there are the fertiliser trucks,' he continued. 'These hills are topdressed most economically from the air, and the fertiliser is brought in to the airstrips in trucks. Cattle trucks, of course, are frequent—double-deckers with a trailer, usually.'

'I think you're trying to frighten me,' she responded coolly. 'No doubt one gets used to anything in time.'

'And no doubt money is a great sweetener.' Strong tanned hands turned the wheel into a gateway lined with rounded trees, conifers of a type unknown to Arminel, their stiff drab olive leaves like tiny spears in the sunlight.

'Te Nawe,' he said calmly, as if he hadn't just insulted her. 'The homestead is half way up the hill.'

Arminel bit her lip as she looked around. First there were buildings, a great woolshed painted dull green, a whole complex of implement barns and yards and pens, a row of dog kennels and then, higher up, two houses which were comfortably embowered in well-established gardens.

Farther on, the homestead was situated on a plateau about three acres in extent, a big, sprawling building in Victorian style, with verandahs and bow windows and interesting little nooks surmounted by a folly of a tower which looked out beyond the fertile lands to the sea.

Arminel drew a deep breath as she leaned forward, her lips parted, for it was like a vision seen through a cascade of pink and white blossom, magnolia trees as big as oaks, their magnificent chalices held up to the blue spring sky, peach blossom and the white airy elegance of plum blossom. Beside the drive fluttered the dancing grace of a bank of lilac primulas, candelabra of blossom swaying gently.

Whoever had planted these gardens had known of the heart-lifting effect of clouds of blossom after the dreariness of winter. Arminel mentally saluted her—or him.

The drive wound around the front of the house, but Kyle took another turning alongside the building, coming to a halt in a large garage which, with the house formed two sides of a wide, paved courtyard. Spring flowers bloomed in gay beds, softening the weatherboard walls of the house and garage. From somewhere the scent of daphne was spicily fragrant on the cool air.

Arminel got herself out of the car, noting with some awe that the garage also sheltered another, smaller car as well as a mud-splattered Land Rover. What few things Rhys had let fall about his life had not prepared her for this untrammelled wealth. For a moment she almost turned back, but a glance at Kyle Beringer's closed face as he took her suitcase from the boot stiffened her resolution. Rich or not, they were just people, she thought sturdily, and certainly Rhys had no snobbish objections to her on her background.

'Ready?'

For what? The guillotine? The strain was making her frivolous, and that she could not afford. Nodding, she fell into place beside him, feeling very small and insignificant against his tall, lean frame.

The door was opened just as they came to it; opened by a rather thin woman with a permanent groove between her brows and eyes which were trying very hard not to show their owner's avid curiosity.

Certainly not Mrs Beringer.

'This is Arminel,' Kyle Beringer introduced with offhanded courtesy. 'Arminel, this is Judy Caird who runs the homestead.'

They murmured greetings, shook hands and then Mrs Caird said briskly, 'Your mother is waiting.'

'Then will you take Arminel to meet her while I put her suitcase away?'

'Of course.' As he turned away Mrs Caird reminded him, 'In the gold bedroom, Kyle.' He nodded and she turned back to Arminel. 'This way, Miss Lovett.'

The house was beautiful, old and spacious, with high ceilings and walls panelled by a warm amber wood. In the wide hall a great chandelier hung like a sunburst, a modern thing which was perfectly at home in its mellow surroundings. A tall Korean chest stood against the wall, its brass hinges and fastenings not gleaming any brighter than the patina on the wood, dark yet glowing. Arminel tried not to look around her in ill-bred curiosity, but when her eye was caught by a landscape her steps slowed and her head turned.

'Nice, isn't it,' Mrs Caird observed. 'Kyle bought it. He buys quite a few paintings. Some people think it's too bare, but that's what the country is like around here.'

Arminel nodded, remembering the high, swooping lines of the hills they had just passed through, the grassy slopes that looked too steep for anything but goats to keep their feet.

The painter had caught the spirit of the landscape, the uncompromising strength and vigour of it, refining the shapes and colours, freeing it of all extraneous detail. It had power and respect, and love of a kind, too.

'We'd better get going,' Mrs Caird said briskly.

The room where her hostess waited was at least twice the size of the sitting rooms Arminel had been accustomed to. Its light, sunny atmosphere didn't really

impinge, for her glance was caught and held by the
woman who rose to greet her, setting aside an
exquisitely worked tapestry as she did so. For a
moment they measured each other, the tall woman in
possession, the interloper, until Mrs Beringer said in a
voice as colourless and cold as a mountain stream,

'Welcome to Te Nawe, Arminel. Did you have a
good flight over?'

'A bit bumpy, but otherwise fine, thank you.'

Obviously Mrs Beringer was not going to let her
disapproval get in the way of the courtesies. Arminel
was not to be outdone. 'It's very kind of you to have
me,' she murmured, wondering how eyes which were
exactly the same colour as Rhys's could be so totally
lacking in warmth and sparkle.

'Not at all. I hope you enjoy your holiday here.'

Well, that put her in her place. 'I'm sure I shall,' she
replied.

Her unwilling hostess turned to the housekeeper,
'Miss Lovett must be impatient for some tea.'

'I'll go and bring it in,' Mrs Caird promised, and
went out, leaving Arminel feeling rather ridiculously as
though her only friend had betrayed her. Not that Mrs
Caird had been particularly welcoming, but at least she
hadn't radiated hostility like the Beringers.

'Do sit down, Arminel.'

Mrs Beringer waited until Arminel sat down in a
small, rather uncomfortable armchair before seating
herself. Then she drew her tapestry into her lap and
applied herself to it for a fraught few seconds before she
looked up sharply, observing,

'You're extremely pretty, Arminel. Rhys has been
singing your praises since he arrived back, but when
Rhys is in the throes of a love affair he tends to see the
whole world through rosy glasses. I believe he said you
work in an office.'

It would be stupid to lose her temper at this none
too subtle put-down. Arminel willed a smile to her

face. 'I work for a lawyer.'

Had. She'd had to resign her job, and right now that seemed the most stupid thing she'd ever done.

'Interesting,' Mrs Beringer said, meaning how incredibly boring and lower class. 'With your looks, surely you could find yourself something a little more glamorous. Modelling perhaps?'

'I like my work,' Arminel returned with calm poise.

Mrs Beringer inclined her head gravely and resumed her stitching. 'You don't sound Australian.'

'My parents were Devon-born.'

'That would explain it, then. I believe Rhys mentioned that you're an orphan.'

'I don't know.' Sparks kindled deep in the cool blue depths of Arminel's eyes, sparks which she kept hidden by demurely lowered lashes. This total lack of welcome chilled and frightened her, but anger smoothed over the cold desolation she was beginning to feel, warming her and giving her confidence.

'Oh?' Beautifully formed brows lifted slightly.

'My parents abandoned me, in their separate and individual ways,' Arminel told her crisply.

The older woman made a distasteful motion with her mouth. 'Dear me! How—how irresponsible of them.'

'I'm afraid they must have both been irresponsible,' Arminel agreed cheerfully. If she could only summon up some remnants of her sense of humour she might yet ride this inquisition. But oh, her heart cried, Rhys, why didn't you tell me?

'So you grew up in an orphanage?'

'More or less.'

'Tragic.' The tapestry was laid aside as Mrs Caird came into the room bearing a tray set with an impressive array of silver and china, which she set down on a table beside Mrs Beringer. There were three cups, so Kyle was going to join them. No doubt he would join his mother in trying to make this intruder feel suitably inferior and chastened.

Sure enough he arrived just after Mrs Caird left, his deep tones in the hall were heard as he said something to her before he pushed the door open and came in.

Arminel's glance flicked across the room, rested on him, then jerked away. He had changed from the dark business suit to casual clothes, trousers and a faintly striped shirt that revealed a splendid body. He owed nothing to his tailor; his masculine presence seemed to fill the room, virile, dominating, intensely dangerous.

Arminel took a sip of tea to moisten her dry mouth and waited for him to join his mother in the attack.

He nodded aloofly to her, and as he accepted a cup from his mother he asked, 'Where's Rhys?'

'Over at Sandiman's, shifting the flock to Creek Two. According to the forecast we'll have wind and rain before morning and you did say Sandiman's is too exposed.'

'It is.' He turned his head, addressing Arminel. 'Every paddock is named. Rhys is moving a flock of ewes and young lambs to a more sheltered paddock. When did he leave?'

'About two hours ago,' his mother answered, her voice without expression. 'He should be back soon.' She sent a calm look across at Arminel. 'The men work very long hours, quite often out before breakfast and not back until it's dark. This is a busy time of year for us. Of course all times are busy, but spring especially so. Tell me, Arminel, do you ride?'

It was asked in exactly the same tone of voice in which her son had wanted to know if she drove. With an effort of will Arminel refrained from looking his way.

'No,' she said. 'I've never been on a horse in my life.' And was not mad keen to try, but that she didn't say.

'Oh dear,' Mrs Beringer remarked, just failing to hide her satisfaction. 'I'm afraid that will limit your excursions quite considerably. Te Nawe is well roaded, of course, but a lot of it is so steep that we still rely on horses to get around. It sounds as though you'll be tied to the homestead. I hope you don't get bored with our quiet life.'

'I'm never bored,' Arminel told her, anger making her reckless. 'I find humanity too fascinating a study to become bored. And I enjoy long walks. Of course, I hope you will allow me to help you in any way I can. I assume that Mrs Caird doesn't do everything?'

A large diamond flashed as Mrs Beringer's fingers closed tightly on to the handle of her teacup. In a voice which for once had some emotion in it she said, 'No, of course not. Like all old places the homestead needs constant upkeep. I'm sure I could find things for you to do, although one must be careful. It's full of treasures.'

'I learn quickly,' Arminel told her. The tea was hot and necessary, giving her something to do with her hands. Probably that was why Mrs Beringer had decided to sew her tapestry; it gave her a subtle advantage.

'Do have something to eat,' her hostess said. 'You're very thin, aren't you? Do you have to diet all the time to keep your figure?'

'No. And no, thank you, I won't eat now. You know how it is flying, they press food on to you whether you want it or not. If I am to eat dinner I'd better abstain now, although it looks delicious.'

As she spoke Arminel looked across at Kyle Beringer, meeting his sardonic scrutiny with cool composure. He was no help, but it seemed that he must have some rudimentary sense of fair play, because he wasn't joining his mother in the attack.

After a long moment's calm eye contact she lowered her lashes, angry because he frightened her. Mrs Beringer was someone she could cope with; it would not be pleasant living in such close proximity to a woman who was a howling snob. However, she would manage. But Kyle Beringer exuded a kind of subtle menace which set her nerves on edge, fretting and tearing at her poise so that she was too acutely aware of him on the periphery of her vision, watchful, his hard narrowed gaze never straying far from her face.

Fortunately now he and his mother spoke of other things; apparently he had been away from home for a few days and was now catching up on what had happened in his absence. Then, when the tea was drunk, Mrs Beringer suggested that she show Arminel her room, sweeping her out of the room and down the hallway.

'Here it is,' she said, pushing the door open. 'I hope you like it. It has its own bathroom, through that door in the far wall. If there's anything you want, you must let me know.'

'Thank you.' Arminel kept her eyes firmly fixed on the older woman as she went on, 'I'll have a shower and a short rest, if I may.'

'Very sensible. We dine about seven-thirty, but someone will come and collect you before then.'

Left alone, Arminel was at last free to allow her eyes to roam the incredible room. Her lips formed a soft whistle as her astounded gaze took in the black wallpaper feathered in gold. On the ceiling, too! Behind the bed was a magnificent, fanciful painting of flowers and wild beasts and people, a mysterious, evocative, vaguely erotic picture in vivid, exciting colours. The bed was an enormous double affair, fourposted, to show off a bedspread of quilted velvet, handmade from scraps of gold, black and scarlet material. Only the neutral gold curtains and black carpet provided any relief from the riot of colour and pattern, as well as two more exquisite Korean chests in black and gold.

It was a fantasy room, gay, brash, overwhelming. Whoever had decorated it had a strong sense of humour and an unerring eye for colour and texture and proportion. As well as a taste for the tactile and stimulating, Arminel decided, looking from that warmly sensuous painting to the seductive bedcover, the lush sensuality of the room. Welcoming, it possessed an aphrodisiac quality which she found strangely pleasurable.

Not a room to relax in, unless it was in the sweet aftermath of desire. A sudden terrifying image of herself and Kyle Beringer entwined in passion on the bed made her catch her breath in shock. Hot coins of colour sprang into her cheeks before she banished the thought. Her subconscious mind must be playing up because she felt threatened by him; if she kept this up she'd be paranoid by the time she left!

Hastily she unpacked her clothes, then, sponge bag in hand, made her way into the bathroom. It had been decorated with the same exuberant imagination, an identical sexy luxury. A peep into the cupboard revealed soaps and shampoos and bath oils, expensive, famous names. Well, they could keep them—she'd use her own far from expensive, but just as efficient, brand.

As she showered she found herself wondering who had decorated this exotic little enclave in a house which, as far as she had seen, was far more formally and conventionally furnished. Certainly not Mrs Beringer, unless she had some interesting quirks in her character! These two rooms revealed a warm, humorous outlook that appealed immensely to Arminel.

Later, relaxed and warm and glowing, wrapped in a quilted dressing gown, she drifted round her room admiring the scarlet and gold tulips in a bronze vase the exact colour of Kyle's hair, the immense maidenhair fern that queened it over a corner, some carvings in stone with a distinctly Eastern look. In another corner a bookshelf held a collection of old favourites and some new, and there was a magazine stand with exactly the sort of magazines Mrs Beringer would take, fashion and the more opulent decorating ones. All very up-market. Nothing geared to the young and poverty-stricken, Arminel decided with a wry smile.

Then tiredness, and the almost intolerable strain

which had her in its grip since she had first met Kyle
Beringer's inimical gaze, made her yawn. Within a few
minutes she was curled up in the bed, sound asleep.

A faint, insistent sound summoned her back.
Opening her eyes, she stared for a few moments in
bewilderment at the ceiling before realising that
someone was knocking impatiently on her door.

Hastily, because it would be Rhys, she hauled her
dressing gown on and flew across to open it, her
expression alight with pleasure and anticipation.

'Darling!' he exclaimed, and caught her in his arms
and kissed her with an eagerness that only intensified
her caution.

His mouth was very sweet and she responded to it
with more than her usual ardour, lifting her hands to
cradle his face, sighing when he groaned, 'Oh, it's been
too long. Too long, my darling girl. Let me look at
you,' as he held her away from him.

'I've only just woken up,' she protested, laughing,
her mouth crimson as a petal. 'I must look a wreck!'

'You always look perfect.' His expression was a
compound of need and impatience; in his jaw a muscle
flicked as he went on, 'Oh, but I've missed you! God,
I'm glad you're here!'

From behind came a voice, drawling, with a steely
note of contempt threaded beneath the surface
mockery.

'As she's going to be here for some days yet why
don't you let her get dressed?'

Instantly Rhys's hands clenched on to her elbows, but
as if he was obliged to obey his brother they loosened
and fell to his sides.

'Sorry, darling,' he said, ignoring Kyle, who had
stopped close behind him and was standing with his
eyes fixed on Arminel's face. As she lifted her chin
defiantly they swept her body, lingering on the delicate
swell of her breasts until she felt as though the dressing
gown was transparent.

'I'll come and get you in ten minutes,' said Rhys, still watching her with that odd hungry look.

Kyle lifted her brows. 'Give her time to put her face on,' he said blandly. 'Make it half an hour.'

'Make it ten minutes,' Arminel countered, smiling very sweetly at Rhys. 'I'll be ready.'

She was, too, but only just, for she had no idea what sort of clothes she would be expected to wear to dinner in this sort of household. Not full evening gear, surely, but most certainly not slacks and a blouse.

In the end she compromised by donning a shirt-dress in flame-coloured jacquard with a small standing collar which emphasised the pale gold sweep of her throat. Long, full sleeves were caught into a cuff at the wrist. A wide gold belt revealed her narrow waist and with it she wore two thick slave bracelets of gilded wood, matching them to gold earrings, long and flamboyant. The temptation to colour her mouth flame was bypassed. She did not want to resemble a scarlet woman! So she made up carefully, touching her lips with gloss over a subdued lipstick, using a faint hint of gold eyeshadow while thanking the good fairy who had handed her out lashes that were thick and black and long. They didn't curl like Rhys's or his brother's, both of whom had an even more beneficent good fairy, but she didn't have to wear mascara.

Perfume? Her one extravagance. Most of her clothes were of her own making, including the dress she wore now; one thing her foster-mother had insisted on was that all the girls who passed through her care should learn how to sew. Arminel was not exactly enamoured of the occupation, but she was good at it and it enabled her to dress smartly for much less cost than her clothes appeared to be worth. This one tonight was a classic pattern, undating, yet it did things for her hair and skin and body.

A finger touched the small bottle of her favourite

perfume and she smiled dreamily as the exquisite top note of 'Ivoire' floated past her nostrils. For tonight she would be exotic, as exotic and flamboyant as this bedroom she had fallen in love with.

# CHAPTER THREE

SHE had chosen well. Mrs Beringer was formal in black silk which was saved from severity by its superb cut and the flattering draped neckline. She looked exactly what she was, a matron of undoubted power and character, her white hair not detracting from the youthful face beneath it. In her ears she wore what were almost certainly real diamond studs, and above her wedding ring there glittered a large but by no means ostentatious diamond.

Courteous but remote, she followed her elder son's lead, using her good manners as a weapon to emphasise the distance that separated them, the wealthy, cultured mature woman and the girl with no background.

With a glass of dry white wine in her hand—a glass?—an exquisite goblet—Arminel was unable to respond to Rhys's attempts to lighten the atmosphere. The air was spiky with tension which neither Mrs Beringer nor Kyle made any attempt to dispel.

Within minutes Rhys fell silent. His mother stepped into the breach by putting Arminel through an inquisition which was as impertinent as it was politely phrased. More stress on the gap between the girl with nothing and the family who had everything.

Calling on all the charity in her soul, Arminel decided that given a similar situation she, too, would want to know the background of her son's girl-friend. So she answered calmly and with precision, ignoring both Rhys's gathering frustration and his brother's watchfulness. She managed to slip a reassuring smile at Rhys, willing him not to explode with the sulky resentment that showed so plainly in his face. Once she looked across the room to where Kyle stood, leaning on the mantel. As if in response he lifted his glance from the contemplation of the glass he was holding and measured her with a cold, dispassionate scrutiny that raised the fine body hairs on her skin.

Fight or flee, she thought ironically. Not for her retreat, the easy way out. Self-respect demanded otherwise. The dark blue of her gaze hardened into defiance. Kyle's brows lifted, then he smiled with merciless directness, his glance shifting from her face to that of the man beside her.

Shaken by emotions she didn't understand, Arminel looked down. Her fingers were pressed so hard against the fragile crystal that the skin was blanched. She felt jumpy and nervous until Mrs Beringer began to speak again, directing the conversation into more general areas.

Then she relaxed, absorbed by a brilliant performance. Once more her hostess was marking out boundaries, and doing it with skill and subtlety. Names were lightly dropped, events recalled and anticipated, people described to Arminel in throwaway phrases— Mrs Beringer was making it more than clear that she and her sons moved in social circles so far removed from Arminel's that they might have lived on the moon.

Again, in spite of the fact that she appreciated exactly what the older woman was doing, Arminel could find it in her heart to sympathise with her. It was clear that she saw in Arminel a threat. Although she was a crashing snob she was fighting for her son's happiness in the only way she knew.

I should be flattered, Arminel thought wryly. Especially as she was by no means certain that whatever she had felt for Rhys was still alive.

Beneath her lashes her glance flicked to him and then, reluctantly, to his brother. Beside Kyle Rhys seemed—very young, very easily read.

'We have very dear friends with an apartment in Surfers.' Mrs Beringer's voice was as smooth and bland as cream. 'I don't suppose you know them—the Rattrays. It was their daughter Davina who persuaded Rhys to take his holiday there. They even lent him their apartment. Wasn't it kind of them?'

'Charming,' Arminel replied. Beside her Rhys shifted position. 'No, I don't know them. Surfers is full of people who come for holidays. Quite a few of them are New Zealanders.'

Somehow her eyes caught Kyle's. She met their silvery glitter with an equanimity she hoped he didn't see through. She would not be intimidated by him, or his mother with her prattle of Governor-Generals and millionaires and famous people.

'Davina is a darling,' Mrs Beringer pursued, worrying at the subject with a surprising lack of finesse. 'I'm sure you'll like her, Arminel.'

Want to bet? Arminel thought drily.

But Rhys moved again, a sudden sharp jerk, before asking heavily, 'Is she coming up?'

'Why, yes, darling.' His mother's smile was tolerant. 'I told you, she's going to spend a month or so with us. Rhys, you must remember! Her letter came—oh, just after you came back from Australia.'

'No, I don't remember.' But he covered his tension and the smouldering anger Arminel could feel by draining his glass, then staring moodily into it, his long fingers turning it restlessly so that the crystal sparkled in a series of little rainbows.

Arminel's lashes drooped. She had noted the sardonic smile that twisted Kyle's mouth at his mother's explanation. She had lied, and he knew it. Clearly Davina Rattray had some part in Rhys's life. Or his mother wanted her to, and wasn't above lying to achieve the results she was after. In her way Mrs Beringer was as ruthless as her older son.

Arminel felt a sudden weariness ache in her bones. More than anything she longed to be back in the flat she shared with three friends. Old and shabby, it cost far too much, but compared to this place with its tangled motives it began to resemble its own sort of Paradise.

Her thoughts were interrupted by Kyle's bland voice. 'Can I get you another drink, Miss Lovett?'

'No, thank you.'

Half laughing, trying hard for a lighthearted tone, Rhys blustered, 'Oh, for heaven's sake, call her Arminel! Once you've said it several times it doesn't sound so weird.'

Kyle stared at her, face impassive except for the mockery that gleamed beneath his lashes. Arminel hesitated. Even this frail barrier was better than none, but with Rhys watching her she could do nothing but second his request.

'Then you must call me Kyle,' he responded, the deep tones revealing nothing but detached courtesy.

Yet he was taunting her; she could feel it vibrating in the air between them, an antagonism that frightened her but was exhilarating too, making her conscious of every nerve and cell in her body, quickening the beat of her heart, the tide of sensation across her skin.

It was a relief when Mrs Caird announced dinner. Such awareness was dangerous, a perilous regression to all that was primitive and untamed in her. Animal magnetism, Arminel thought scornfully as Rhys escorted her into the big shadowy dining room. Both brothers possessed it, that basic unregenerate attraction, but in Rhys it was a muted version of his brother's. Some time she would try to fathom out exactly what it was which pulled her so strongly that she was acutely conscious of Kyle, seeing him even when she looked elsewhere.

Above the softly gleaming table a lamp hung, high enough to illuminate the centrepiece of orchids, the crystal and china and silver, low enough to enclose them in its pool of mellow light.

Mrs Beringer unfolded her napkin, the diamond on her finger flashing as her voice flowed out gently.

The food was superbly cooked and beautifully presented. Arminel ate it without appetite, sure that she was disappointing her unwilling hostess by using the correct knives and forks.

What a silly woman, she thought tiredly. Surely she realises that nowadays even little office girls dine in good restaurants! Mrs Beringer's view of the world, one rigidly divided into classes, went out a century or so ago. If New Zealand was anything like Australia such a system had never really taken root. Oh, there were classes, but passage from one to the other was easy enough. Two generations with money, the right schools and an investment in social life was all that it took, she thought, unaware that the cynical little thought was reflected in her face.

From behind Mrs Beringer a portrait stared down at them. At first Arminel had thought it was a likeness of Kyle, but several surreptitious glances convinced her otherwise. Every bit as handsome as Kyle, the subject was dressed in Victorian clothes and wore a Victorian expression of stern superiority. He had been painted by someone with skill enough to suggest an imperious character with more than a hint of implacable authority.

Obviously an ancestor. Her eyes discerned in the background a familiar silhouette with the scar of the landslide faithfully rendered, so whoever he was he had lived here. Curiosity impelled her to ask how long the family had been at Te Nawe.

She addressed the question to Rhys, but he disclaimed knowledge with a shrug. 'Ask Kyle, he's the expert on family history.'

So Arminel was forced to look across to where his brother sat back in his chair. The lamplight burnished his hair to a glowing hue, bronze with russet highlights, emphasising the harsh symmetry of his features and the breadth of shoulders and chest. His expression gave nothing away and it was difficult to see what emotion, if any, irradiated the pale eyes.

An odd tug at Arminel's senses shocked her. With a small sigh of relief she turned her glance to Mrs Beringer, who answered her.

'Over a hundred and fifty years, a long time.'

'It certainly is for such a young country,' Arminel agreed politely. One of the few things she knew about her father's family was that it had been located in the same place in Devon for more than three hundred years. They had been country people, their roots deep in the land that supported them.

The dark lashes of the man opposite her lifted as he sent her a long, considering stare which set her teeth on edge. Deep in some hidden part of her body a sensation unlike anything she had felt before flamed into life. Almost desperately she lifted her glass to her mouth to hide her uneasiness. Above the rim her eyes held his, a challenge implicit in their dark blue depths. For a moment he met it, his gaze very hard and sure, before his eyes dropped to her mouth.

A strange heat prickled across her skin. It was not a blush, more a defensive reaction. Subduing the flare of reaction, she forced herself to smile enquiringly at him.

'That must have been quite early in the pioneering days, surely?'

'Early enough,' said Kyle in his deep voice, still watching the movement of her lips as she spoke.

Mrs Beringer laughed. 'Both the Beringers and my family were early settlers,' she said quite pleasantly. 'But my side were a stolid, respectable lot who arrived in Christchurch on the first four ships before taking up land in the mountains. Dull. I like the sound of the first Kyle Beringer. He was a pirate.'

'Literally?'

Kyle answered Arminel's lifted brows with a thin smile. 'No, not literally, but definitely black sheep material. He skipped from his father's manor in England after seducing the daughter of a minor noble. Some time later she disappeared too, eventually turning up here as his wife. In the intervening years he'd spent a while in Australia before sailing across the Tasman to make his home with the tribe who at that time owned Te Nawe and the surrounding area. He was given the nucleus of the station; it took him thirty years and the use of means fortunately unknown to his descendants to acquire the rest.'

'He sounds a fascinating scoundrel,' said Arminel, her slow smile irradiating her face. Without the tight mask of control which she had worn since first setting eyes on Kyle her beauty came swiftly to provocative life, a fugitive dimple giving her a young, vulnerable air.

It affected them all in their various ways, although none but Rhys showed it. For the first time he relaxed, lifting his chin to stare at his brother in a mixture of pride and belligerence. Kyle looked at him, revealing nothing.

'He was.' Mrs Beringer hurried into speech. 'Hard as nails and laden with charm. But he was a good husband. All the records show how devoted he was to both of his wives.'

'Simultaneous or successive?' Arminel asked.

Rhys gave a crack of laughter. 'Clever darling! Got it one. Simultaneous. One was the granddaughter of the local chief. Her father was an American whaler. Our revered ancestor got the first part of Te Nawe through her.'

Arminel's eyes danced in quick response. 'He sounds fascinating. How did he keep order?'

'With a whip, if family legend is based on truth.' Kyle looked as though he thoroughly agreed with his ancestor's methods, his handsome features ironic. 'Each wife had a child. About two generations later the heir to each side married, uniting the family again.'

Arminel observed drily, 'Sensible of them. He must have been a remarkable man. One can only admire his stamina.'

'You must get Kyle to tell you some of the stories

about him,' Mrs Beringer said graciously, adding with a twinkle that made her seem much more human, 'He was probably the sort of person one wouldn't allow over one's threshold now. It's because we're safely out of his reach that we enjoy him so.'

Well, yes. Although Arminel was prepared to bet that while Kyle was alive his ancestor couldn't really be called dead and gone. Like the man in the portrait, he possessed a disturbing sensuality. It took no imagination at all to see him coping more than adequately with two wives, calming any quarrels with the cold whip of his gaze. Just as feminine instinct told her that his virility would be more than capable of meeting any demands made on it.

Such thoughts were dangerous. She banished them, glad that dinner was over. With any luck he would go and find some office work to do. Surely rich station owners spent hours poring over figures, totting up the profits from their endeavours?

But he went with them back into the room where they had gathered before dinner. While Rhys piled driftwood on to the fire and his mother turned the television on Kyle picked up a book and sat down in an armchair some distance away.

Rhys pulled Arminel down beside him on to the sofa, his possessive hand over hers as he bent his attention to the screen. The comic was clever, the skits amusing and thought-provoking, but from the corner of her eye Arminel caught the quick flick of pages as Kyle read, lean fingers on white paper, long legs stretched casually in front of him. If he was reading, not just skimming, he had an incredible speed.

Arminel moved restlessly, forcing her gaze back to the screen. Beside her Rhys chuckled; his mother laughed out loud. The fire crackled, spat and then hissed as the flames released a pocket of air. Arminel's eyes moved to the incisive profile of the man in the armchair.

Halfway through her appraisal he glanced up. Something kindled in his face as their eyes met. Whatever it was it was rapidly suppressed, but he held her gaze while a small grim smile gave his face an almost sinister cast.

Hurriedly Arminel looked away, lashes lowered to hide the dilation of her pupils. Her tongue touched suddenly dry lips. She could feel his eyes on her and wondered if he had felt the impact of her gaze as though it was a branding-iron.

'Relax,' Rhys whispered, squeezing her tense fingers.

It was impossible. She was too conscious of the electric tingle across her face and throat which meant that Kyle had not returned to his reading.

When the last peals of laughter from the television audience had died away Rhys turned to her. 'I suppose you're tired. Do you want an early night?'

In a low voice she said, 'We've got to talk, Rhys.'

He nodded, unable to hide the wariness her words caused. 'Yes, sure. Come on.'

No one said anything as they left the room, although Arminel knew that two pairs of eyes followed them. As the door closed she heard Mrs Beringer break into speech. Suddenly cold, she shivered.

'Poor darling,' Rhys commiserated, sliding his arm around her waist. 'Poor cold darling! When I got back from Surfers I thought I was never going to get warm again!'

'There is a difference,' she agreed, unable to tell him that her fit of shivering had nothing to do with temperature.

He took her into a room lined with books, furnished with a buttoned leather sofa and armchairs covered in pleasantly mellow material, green and rose and amber.

'Now, how are you?' he asked in a suddenly thickened voice as he pulled her roughly into his arms. 'Oh, God, I've missed you! It's been hell. . . .'

His mouth closed over hers, coaxing, pleading for a response which she realised now she could not give him.

But she kissed him back because she liked his mouth
on hers and because he was the only person this side of
the Tasman Sea who liked her.

'That's better,' he sighed, lifting his head to smile
down at her. 'Why, darling, you're crying! What is it?'

'Not crying.' But her lashes were wet. 'Why didn't
you tell me how things were here, Rhys?'

'What do you mean?'

Her mouth firmed as she looked levelly at him, seeing
the quick evasion in his expression. 'You know. Neither
your mother nor your brother want me here. If I'd
known——'

'You wouldn't have come,' he interrupted. 'That's
why, idiot.'

'But *why*, Rhys? Why do they dislike me?'

His uncertainty was plain to read. After a moment he
groaned, 'Oh, hell, I knew you'd be mad, love, but I had to
have you here. Sit down, let me hold you, while I explain.'

'It had better be good,' she said, but she allowed him
to scoop her against his side as they sat on the sofa. For
a moment Rhys was silent, his arm tense about her
shoulder.

'I'm sorry,' he began, kissing her unresponsive cheek.
'So sorry, but in a way, darling, you can't blame Kyle
and Mama. I know they've been stiff with you——'

'Stiff?'

'O.K.,' he said sulkily, 'so they've been bloody rude to
you, Mama doing her grande dame act and Kyle
showing you just how overbearing he can be, and I
know, none better, how high-handed he can get, but
they got a considerable shock when I told them I was
going to marry you.'

'You *what*?' Even though she had suspected it his
words still appalled her. She turned her head to stare at
him, saw his shamefaced bravado and bit out, 'Rhys,
how could you? We agreed——'

'Oh, I know you said you'd have to get to know me
better,' he groaned, kissing the tumbling words from

her lips, 'but, Arminel, you felt it just as I did, you fell in love with me, I know you did.'

'How do you know?' Anger glittered in the depths of her eyes, turning them to dark sapphires; it flamed along the high bones of her cheeks. 'Rhys, we agreed that we didn't know each other well enough!'

'No, you said that. I knew.' His voice was positive, almost aggressive. 'The first time I saw you I said to myself, there she is, exactly what you've always promised yourself. I knew you, darling, I know you now. I love you.'

She shook her head, her anger dying in the light of his emotion. 'Oh—oh!' she sighed, 'but don't you see, *I* don't know! I know that I like you immensely; when you kiss me I enjoy it, we have lots of things in common, but I'm not *sure*! And I'm not marrying, not you, not anyone, until I'm absolutely certain.' She looked into his uncomprehending face, saying with complete conviction, 'I'm not going to marry and then find that it was a mistake, as my mother did. No way, Rhys. For me it's going to be marriage for ever, no second thoughts, no divorce.'

'O.K., O.K.,' he said, placating her, taking possession of the hands that gesticulated so fiercely. 'All right, I can understand that. You've had a rough spin and God knows, I want the same as you. But can't you believe that for me that's how it is?'

'Not after three weeks' acquaintance!'

He sighed and lifted her hands to his lips, his expression regaining some of the lighthearted humour which had drawn her so strongly in Surfers.

'Arminel, why not just leave it, hmm? As soon as Kyle and Mama realise that you aren't a gold-digging little—well, aren't anything like that, they'll get to like you, I know they will.'

Arminel sighed, thinking wearily that it seemed centuries ago since she she had flown out of Brisbane so eagerly looking forward to seeing him again.

'Why did you tell them that we were as good as engaged?' she asked, and as his expression hardened into into stubbornness, 'I must know, Rhys, or I'll leave tomorrow.'

He had been holding her hands, running his thumbs over her palms. Now his fingers clenched as his mouth pulled into a straight line. 'Davina Rattray,' he said sulkily.

'Well?'

'Well, Mama has always hoped that Davina and I— that we—oh, you must have guessed! She made it obvious enough! I like Davina, she's a nice kid, but I don't want to marry her.'

'I see.'

'Do you?' He released her hands and stood up, a frown pulling his brows together. 'I doubt if you do. You've no idea what it's been like for the last year. Every time I turn around there she is. If I flirt with another girl she looks reproachful and sad. Hell, it's beyond bearing! Mama has done her work so well that we get invited everywhere as a pair. I feel as though I'm being slowly and steadily forced into marriage.'

'Why don't you discuss it with the girl, tell her that you like her but that's all?'

Rhys exhibited all the classic signs of the male at a disadvantage, shrugging as though his collar was too tight, hands shoved forcefully into his pockets.

'Oh, because—well, it's so bloody embarrassing,' he said at last, defensively. 'I like her, she's a pretty little thing and she's in love with me. I don't want to hurt her. I just wish she'd leave me alone. And now Mama has invited her up!'

He swung around to stare accusing at Arminel as if she had been a party to the invitation. 'I won't be able to turn round without tripping over her. I've had enough! That's why I said—I let Kyle and Mama believe that we were engaged.'

Arminel frowned. She saw much more than he knew;

he certainly wasn't in love with her, no more than he was with poor Davina Rattray. Harried by his mother's relentless pressure, he was prepared to use her as a shield against a marriage he was not ready for.

And she? Without much surprise she realised that whatever she had felt for Rhys had evaporated like bubbles from flat champagne. Their romance had been a classic holiday affair, all rainbows and fun, gilded with the sun, nurtured by his holiday mood and her need for someone to love her. The sensation of loss gave her a pang of melancholy; it had been lovely and now it was dead. But that was all.

Not that Rhys was ready to accept reality. Shrewdly she appreciated that while he could continue to use her as a buffer he would believe that he loved her, his self-esteem would insist on that. Only love, she thought cynically, could sweeten such exploitation.

'You're an idiot,' she said, but without rancour.

He grinned and came back to sit beside her, possessing himself once more of her hands. 'And you're a darling. A very lovable darling.'

'But I'm still angry,' she said, forestalling an attempt to kiss her. 'You've no right to drag me into all this, and you know it!'

'But you're not going to tell them that we aren't engaged?'

'No, you are.'

It took him twenty minutes of coaxing before she reluctantly capitulated, and even then her motives were distinctly mixed. Some unregenerate part of her was maliciously pleased at the idea of infuriating Mrs Beringer and Kyle; it would be satisfying to make them suffer a little. But her main reason for agreeing to the deception was a kind of confused loyalty to Rhys. He had all of the stubbornness of the innately weak, but she could see that he wasn't going to be able to hold out much longer against the kind of pressure to which he was being subjected. Possibly Davina Rattray was the perfect choice for him, but he should be the one who made the choice, not his mother, nor his brother, or their friends.

For although he said that Kyle had made no attempt to persuade him into this marriage it was quite obvious that he was all for it. Otherwise why should he have seen Arminel as a threat? No, Kyle was too astute to subject Rhys to the kind of coercion his mother used, but there were other, more subtle means of persuasion.

She sighed, frowning. Perhaps if they realised that this time they had pushed Rhys too hard they might in future ease up and allow him to make his own decisions. In a way she felt obliged to accede to his request, though her very instinct warned her that she was a fool, the safest and most sensible thing to do would be to get as far away from Te Nawe and Kyle Beringer as possible.

'Oh—very well,' she said crossly.

'You're a sweetie!' Rhys whispered jubilantly, kissing her with expert panache.

She laughed, knowing perfectly well that he was using her, content for it to be so. It wasn't Rhys's fault that he had a domineering mother and a brother who possessed a dark male beauty that drew the eye and the senses. No wonder Rhys was overshadowed! The virility and effortless authority which were so basic a part of Kyle's character would overwhelm any other man—and appeal to that primitive core hidden deep in all women which yearned to be protected and dominated. Although she disliked him immensely, Arminel recognised the strength he possessed. Put simply, if she was being menaced by a dragon or kidnapped by spacemen, it would be to Kyle that she would look for aid, not Rhys. And that was not Rhys's fault.

When he saw the faint smile which accompanied this thought he grinned and kissed her again, his mouth warm and sensuous as it moved over hers.

'I'm glad you're not too mad at me,' he whispered.

'We'll play it your way, I promise, not too heavy, but I'm going to convince you that we'll be happy together.'

As she pulled away Arminel found herself thinking wryly that Rhys was as little accustomed as his brother to being rebuffed. He might not have the magnetic attraction that marked Kyle out from the rest of the human race, but his good looks and that smooth gloss of sophistication and wealth and self-confidence must have made it an unusual thing for him to be rejected by any girl he fancied. Unless the girl was already in love with his brother. But somehow Arminel felt that Rhys would not be attracted to women who had their eyes set on Kyle. He must know that the competition was too fierce.

She should, of course, be furious with him for using her as a shield against the importunate Davina Rattray, but she could understand only too well why he was so helpless—and so resentful. Kyle Beringer would have been able to rid himself of someone who clung and got in his way. A few brief cold words and that would have been the end of any such entanglement.

But Arminel hated to cause pain, and she liked Rhys all the better because he felt some compunction for the girl who loved him. Not that she agreed with his method of dealing with the situation, but perhaps Rhys saw it more clearly than she. And perhaps it was kinder to convince Davina that he had fallen in love with another girl rather than make it obvious that he just didn't care enough for her.

'Why don't you tell your mother that you're just not interested in marrying Davina?' she asked. 'Surely she doesn't want to push you into a marriage that's almost bound to be unhappy?'

He said sulkily, 'I've told her hundreds of times, but she just sighs and says Davina is perfect for me. She won't take any notice. In some ways she's like Kyle, totally ruthless, only Mama never loses her temper. Anyway, it won't take them long to come round,' he went on, speaking with a cheerful lack of concern. 'Mama wants me to be happy, and when she sees that you make me happy she'll ease up. And Kyle doesn't really care. He doesn't think much of women anyway, except as girl-friends.'

Clearly Mrs Beringer was right when she said that Rhys viewed the world through rose-coloured spectacles. He certainly suffered from selective vision, seeing only what he wanted to see.

Arminel repressed a shiver as she recalled that first sight of Kyle Beringer, tall and uncompromisingly arrogant, cold eyes surveying her with autocratic disdain. Given time Mrs Beringer might accept Arminel as a member of the family, but Kyle never would. He was like a statue carved by a master, beautiful, forceful, and stone to the core.

'You make him sound like a proper chauvinist,' she said, wondering why she should feel any curiosity at all.

'Oh, he's that, all right. Not that he thinks women are an inferior sex, or anything, because he doesn't. His girl-friends are all clever, usually frighteningly so. But he's not keen on getting married. He said once that women want too much and he's not prepared to spend any time pandering to their basic insecurity.' He grinned at her expression and dropped a kiss beneath her ear, murmuring, 'But why talk about him? He's . . .'

Of course the door opened at just that moment to let Kyle in. When he saw them he smiled, not pleasantly, his brows climbing as he surveyed Arminel's flush and her quick withdrawal.

'Do you mind?' Rhys blustered, releasing her before he got to his feet.

'Not at all.' His brother sounded bored, but the pale eyes didn't leave Arminel's face. 'Do you think you could make love somewhere else? I've work to do. Mama is still watching television, but the rest of the house is unoccupied.'

Sarcastic swine! Why did he keep staring as if he was trying to pierce her brain with his eyes?

'Sorry.' Rhys bent to pull Arminel up. 'Say goodnight to Kyle, darling.'

The rather too pronounced note of satisfaction in his voice attracted the attention of both of the others in the room. An uneasy sensation niggled at Arminel's composure when she saw the open challenge in the glance he flung towards Kyle; it was not appeased by the long, considering gaze he received in reply.

Then Kyle looked at her, the dark lashes lowering to hide the icy contempt which had slashed across her face and throat.

'Goodnight, Kyle,' she said swiftly.

'Goodnight, Arminel,' he returned, and if there was a mocking note in the deep voice it was almost too well hidden to recognise.

Once outside the room Rhys chuckled soundlessly as he draped an arm about her shoulders, guiding her down the passage towards her room.

'No.' She stopped. 'I'll say goodnight to your mother. They were very keen on manners, my foster-parents.'

He ignored the irony of her smile to say with easy charm, 'Well, they made a success of yours,' as he wheeled her about.

Mrs Beringer had picked up her needlepoint once more. The exchanged goodnights were coolly polite, but the older woman's smile did not ever reach the chilly blue depths of her eyes.

Outside Arminel's room Rhys kissed her again, his mouth ardent and seeking.

'I'm tired,' said Arminal, evading him. Suddenly weary, she weakly put off telling him that she wasn't there to be treated as his girl-friend of the moment.

Once inside the room she decided that probably it would be better not to come out so directly with the truth. She rather suspected that one of the reasons he thought himself in love with her was that she hadn't succumbed completely to his smooth charm. Had she given in to his coaxing and allowed him to become her lover he might even now be wondering what he had seen in her.

Perhaps it was poor Davina Rattray's open love for him that made him so adamant with her. Man, the hunter, Arminel thought, leaning back against the door, and then—well, why not? If Rhys enjoyed the pursuit as much as the kill it would be up to the woman who wanted him to ensure that he never stopped pursuing.

That that woman was not her she was now convinced. As she gazed around the warm, glowing fantasy of her room she found her eyes were wet, and when she tried to chase away her dreariness with a smile it turned out to be a distinctly wobbly one.

'So,' she said severely, scowling, 'so you thought you loved him and you've found out that you don't. Clever you, to make sure before committing yourself.'

But she couldn't help her half-wistful grief at the death of something frivolous and ephemeral but lovely while it lasted. And as she cleaned her face and teeth and brushed her hair she found herself wishing that she hadn't felt almost obliged to agree to Rhys's request to pretend an engagement. A strange, fey instinct warned her that she was courting danger.

Until the cool common sense which was as essential a part of her as the beauty that caught so much attention countered this vague premonition with the brisk reminder that this was New Zealand, not Transylvania. The most dangerous thing that could happen to her was that someone might insist on putting her up on a horse!

The bed had been turned back so that the light shone on percale sheets and pillowcases, luxurious and infinitely welcoming.

Make the most of it, she thought, smiling a little, for in this enticing, opulent room she felt more than a little out of place. Her nightdress was one she had made herself of pale gold lawn in a simple pattern with its only ornament narrow lace edging to the neck and around the hem. Not in the least enticing or luxurious.

A sharp tap at the door made her jump and look wildly across the room.

'Wait a moment!' she called as she made a dive for her dressing gown.

But the door opened instantly and Kyle Beringer walked in. Even when he saw her struggling to drag the dressing-gown over her nightdress he didn't turn away or do anything but look amused. Condescendingly amused. At least, that was his smile. His eyes flicked across her face and then travelled the slender length of her body with insulting thoroughness.

'I said to wait,' she flashed, hauling the belt tight about her narrow waist. Quick heat burned in her cheeks and throat.

'Sorry.' He didn't believe her, but at the sudden tightening of her lips he lifted a hand and drawled, 'No, don't order me out! I'm not going until we've got a few things straight.'

'What things?'

The light licked gleaming flames into the bronze hair as he jerked his head to indicate the room next door. 'I sleep through there,' he said calmly. 'And I'm a light sleeper. I'll leave the door open slightly, so if you're expecting Rhys to come and while away the hours with you, forget it. I'll have him out if I have to drag him out of your arms!'

Swift anger flared in the depths of her eyes. While he talked she had folded her arms defensively across her breasts. Now they dropped to her sides as her hands clenched into small fists. But even as the hot words beat to be free she swallowed them back, breathing deeply before she spoke.

'You needn't bother,' her voice dripped disgust. 'And don't lose sleep listening for footsteps, either. Rhys is not my lover.'

The dark brows lifted in complete, devastating

disbelief. 'Really? He gave me the impression that your relationship was considerably more intimate than that characterised by a chaste goodnight kiss.'

'Then he lied,' she said steadily.

'Possibly.' But he was smiling, his sceptical gaze very insolent as it touched her lips and the expanse of pale skin revealed by the deep neck of her dressing gown, before roaming the swell of her hips and the long line of her legs. 'But Rhys,' he continued, 'is not in the habit of lying. And I happen to know that although he's only twenty-two he's packed a lot of experience in those years.' Hard, cutting as a whip, his gaze flicked up to her face, white now but held proudly.

'And you,' he said pleasantly, as he came towards her, 'are very beautiful.'

Every instinct she possessed urged her to flee, to run before the threat which he offered her. But she could not move.

And when she spoke it was to ask in a kind of croak, 'How old are you?'

He looked amused. 'Twenty-nine. And yes, I've acquired a lot of experience too. One tends to, you know, if one has the money. There are very few women who aren't prepared to sell their virtue—dearly in some cases, but it's usually on offer.'

He was close to her, so close that she thought she could feel the warmth of his body beating against hers. His finger touched her ear, pushing the black drift of silk back from it. Arminel had never thought of the ear as an erogenous zone before; now she realised that when the right man—*no*—when a man of vast experience ran the tip of his finger lightly around the edge, tugged at the lobe and then began to explore the circular crevice—she winced, jerking her head sideways while her breath came in thick short gasps between lips which had fallen a little apart. Strange little rills of pleasure were threading their way along her nerves. Her brain felt woolly and thick, so intent on processing the information her senses were feeding it that it could not think.

'Beautiful,' Kyle repeated, not touching her now but somehow holding her in submission before him. 'With a strange, disturbing, sensual beauty that would tempt a saint. Rhys is no saint. Nor am I.'

It was difficult to concentrate when her eyes told her brain that his shoulders were wide and held tensely, that there was a quality of stillness about the superb athlete's body so close to hers which hinted at the use of great self-control. His warm, tormentingly masculine scent teased her nostrils and intensified the strange mixture of sensations that were crowding in on her. The deep voice played on her nerve-ends; without lifting her eyes she knew that whatever he might think of her he was just as affected as she was by this strange sensual lethargy which held them prisoner.

*I—must—not——* she thought, forcing herself to overcome the shackles of the body. Deliberately she bit her lip until the pain cleared her brain. Then she stepped back, arms once more coming defensively to cover breasts which suddenly seemed heavy.

'Well,' she said, coolly, pleasantly ironic, 'now that you've warned me perhaps you would like to go? I really am quite tired.'

It hurt to look up into his face, see the magnificent bone structure suddenly prominent as the skin above it tightened. Just for a moment something ugly flickered deep in his eyes. Then he smiled and said just as pleasantly, 'Sleep well, Arminel.'

# CHAPTER THREE

SURPRISINGLY she did, waking the next morning to the sound of another tap at the door.

But this one heralded Mrs Caird, bearing a superbly set breakfast tray.

'Oh, but you mustn't,' Arminel protested through her yawns. 'I'll get up. You mustn't go to all this trouble.'

'Well, Mrs Beringer thought that as you'd had a tiring day yesterday this would give you a little longer sleep.'

The housekeeper deposited the tray across Arminel's knees. She didn't exactly smile, but she certainly looked a lot more friendly than she had the day before.

So Arminel smiled warmly and said, 'That looks delicious. Tell me, do the men get eggs Benedict for breakfast as well, or is this just a treat for me?'

'You and Mrs Beringer.' Mrs Caird relaxed even more. 'The men have a proper meal at breakfast time—well, at every mealtime. They work hard.'

She pulled the curtains back to reveal a sunny day outside. Through the French doors there was a terrace of split sandstone bordered by daisies, white and gold and pink, and beyond them a stretch of lawn, tree-shadowed, with a path which led to an arbour hung with the starry white flowers of clematis.

'That's our native one,' said Mrs Caird, following the direction of Arminel's appreciative gaze. 'Pretty, isn't it?'

'It's beautiful. But then New Zealand is beautiful—at least, the little I've seen of it. So green and lush, and so little.'

'Wait till you see the Southern Alps before you talk of size.' But the older woman was not annoyed. She continued, 'Every country has its own beauty. Me, I like the shops in Sydney and Melbourne!'

'Well, yes,' Arminel agreed, smiling. 'Who doesn't?'

'I'll come and collect the tray——'

But Arminel shook her head. 'No, you'll do no such thing! I can find my way back to the kitchen. I don't want to make any extra work.'

That got a faintly sceptical look along with the thanks, which led Arminel to wonder exactly what sort of female guests the Beringers were used to.

As she ate she found herself hoping that after all this might be a pleasant holiday. Certainly the surroundings were beautiful enough to ravish the eye; if she could only tread a careful path through the minefield of human relationships that surrounded her she might yet enjoy herself here. Resolutely pushing away the memory of a perfectly satisfactory job abandoned for a deceptive rainbow trail of romance, she set herself to counting over her blessings. In a way it served her right for being so impulsive. Not even to herself did she admit how much she had wanted to love Rhys; it was easier to think about cutting her losses, repaying Rhys for his hospitality and learning from the situation.

How the rich live! she thought cheerfully; she was never likely to move in circles like this again, so she might as well soak up as many impressions as she could while she was here. Old money, and the house and its occupants revealed it. And if Mrs Beringer was a snob—well, at least she was human enough to enjoy the stories about the first Kyle, who must have been a rip-roaring old reprobate. Two wives!

Chuckling, Arminel slid from the bed and made her way to the bathroom. Half an hour later, dressed in warm slacks and a woollen blouse, for although sunny it was still a lot cooler than at home, she made her bed and tidied away the few signs of her occupancy in both rooms, then opened a French door out on to the terrace. Immediately a large cat, patchworked in an interesting pattern of ginger and black, came purring in.

'Well, hello,' Arminel smiled, bending to rub him in just the right place behind the ears.

'That,' Mrs Caird told her in the kitchen a few minutes later, 'is Smitty. He's not quite sure whether he's a dog or a human being.'

Arminel chuckled as she watched the housekeeper load the dishes into the dishwasher. 'He seems all cat to me.'

'He spends quite a bit of his time down in the yards helping the dogs with the sheep. And he thinks he should have every privilege we have, including bathing in my bath.'

Arminel laughed at the same moment that the door opened.

'Oh, there you are,' came in a masculine voice. 'Would you like to come for a drive? I'm going around the place and Mama thought it would give you some idea of the place if you came with me.'

And got her out of Mrs Beringer's hair. Mrs Caird had already explained that the older woman didn't usually rise until nine or so. But the hair on the back of Arminel's neck rose at the thought of once more sharing the cab of a vehicle with Kyle. After that unsettling scene last night she didn't want ever to see him again.

Still, after a hesitation so slight that she hoped it wasn't noticed, Arminel accepted.

'Then come on,' he said, almost impatient. 'Got that thermos ready, Judy?'

The vehicle that waited was the Land Rover, with two interested dogs in the back.

'Run and get a jacket,' Kyle ordered. 'We're pretty sheltered here, but the wind is keen on the hills.'

He wore jeans and boots and a checked shirt with long sleeves rolled up beyond his elbows to reveal corded muscles. And he looked every inch a sex symbol, Arminel thought reluctantly, hating the effect his intense masculinity had on her. Remember, he thinks you a gold-digging little tramp, she reminded herself.

But it was hard to remember it when from the moment she climbed up into the seat beside him he seemed to set himself out to charm her. And everything was so new, and so interesting, from the great Hereford stud bulls in a paddock close to the house to the gorgeous little white-faced calves and their mothers, so that after a short time she forgot her wariness. Sheep, silly, pretty things on thin legs, grazed in paddock after paddock. Kyle answered her questions with patience, revealed the difference between ewes and wethers and hoggets, and explained the mysteries of docking and crutching and shearing, even appalled her with a quick résumé of the diseases to which sheep were prone.

There was a herd of Angora goats, too, delectable things with enchanting kids which came racing up to greet them when they came into the paddock.

'Oh—oh, how lovely!' Arminel bent to stroke one impatient little head, found another butting at her knee, and two others pushing eagerly for a place.

'Part of a diversification programme,' Kyle said somewhat shortly, his face expressionless as his eyes rested on the vivid, glowing face lifted to his. 'Goats eat stuff the sheep won't touch—gorse, blackberry, weeds of all sorts. We have a milking herd, too; there's a good market for goat milk here in New Zealand and for goat meat in the Pacific.'

She nodded, realising for the first time that a farmer such as Kyle must be part entrepreneur, part man of the land, all combined with a talent for organisation.

Too soon they had to leave the adorable Angoras behind to head on up a narrow but well-made track, one of a system of roads that ran all over the station. As they climbed the sea gradually occupied more of the panorama until Kyle stopped the Land Rover and said simply, 'There.'

Almost half of the horizon was filled by the sea, green and silver-blue, glittering in the rays of the sun. Far, far out in the shining boundary between sea and sky hung the faint blue shapes of islands; to the north the land curved in a series of hills and bays and capes until a blue-purple range of mountains cut off the view.

'Well, hardly mountains,' Kyle told her. 'They're only a thousand or so feet high.'

'Mountains to me, although inland from Surfers the mountains go up to three thousand feet,' she returned.

He grinned, teasing her, hostility forgotten. 'In New Zealand we call them hills until they reach three or four thousand feet.'

She repressed a sudden surge of pleasure perilously akin to delight. 'How high is Te Nawe? The actual hill, I mean.'

'Fifteen hundred feet.'

They were standing on its flank. Above them rose further heights, the stark outline blurred by a thick mantle of rain forest, lush, brooding, almost hiding the scar which had given the hill its name. Below the land fell away in folds and bush-lined gullies, its clean bare lines beautiful and satisfying to the eye.

And filling the lungs was the air, fresh and cool with the rich smell of the bush and the clean crispness of growing things.

'It's beautiful,' said Arminel half beneath her breath. 'It has a kind of awesomeness about it. Did we really come all the way up that tiny track?'

'We did, indeed. You're not afraid of heights?'

She looked at him. 'Apparently not. Why?'

'Quite a few people blench at that track. I've even had to let several out.'

'Is that why we came up here?'

He lifted a quizzical brow at her. 'Now, what reason could I possibly have for frightening you?'

'None, I hope,' she retorted, unable to rid herself of the feeling that he had brought her here for exactly that purpose. Before she could change her mind she asked, 'Where's Rhys today?'

'Suddenly remembered him? He's repairing a fence

down there—you should be able to see him—no, not there. Down there.' He moved behind her, positioned her face in the right direction and pointed, the hard muscle in his arm pushing against her cheek.

For a moment her vision blurred. She could feel his heart beat steadily into her shoulder, was acutely aware that as hers began to pick up speed so did his.

'Yes, I can see,' she said harshly, stepping away from him.

'Can you?'

He was right to sound sceptical, for she was unable to see anything but a vision of herself lost in his arms. Blinking fiercely, she managed to banish it, but the colour that rolled up through her skin could not be controlled so easily.

'Why, Arminel!' his voice mocked, and she felt his hands on her shoulders, turning her to face him.

Perhaps she should not have resisted. Her instinctive withdrawal seemed to act as a goad. The next moment she was enfolded, and Kyle's mouth was moving with practised seduction over hers. It was warm and hard, as pleasant as his brother's, persuasively tempting her to part her lips beneath his.

Arminel jerked her head back, ashamed and disgusted with herself. For a moment she had forgotten Rhys.

'No,' she muttered as his mouth moved erotically over the contours of her face. 'Rhys.'

'Oh, damn Rhys!' he breathed, and when she tried to push him away stopped her by the simple expedient of crushing her lips beneath his in a kiss that forced them apart.

After that intimate, intense exploration she was unable to resist any longer. Indeed, she had no conception of what was happening to her. Reason, logic, even thought fled; she was totally at the mercy of the sensations which he was arousing with his deep kisses and the slow movement of his hands beneath her jacket as he explored the length of her spine before finally pulling her hard against him.

He was as aroused as she; his body was tense, thrusting, making her aware of his hunger and her own wildfire response. And this had never happened before. Dimly she was conscious of the gasping sound that broke from her swollen lips, and then her hands slid across his back and she pressed herself against him, offering him that which she had passively let him take before.

She was trembling, her skin suffused with heat as sensations of indescribable pleasure arose from every nerve end and swamped her in the first real rush of passion she had ever experienced. Opening her eyes, she drowned in the pale blaze of his as their mouths clung in a kiss which forced her head back on to his arm. Then his lips moved to the arc of her throat, the heated pressure tormenting her, making her body ache.

And quite suddenly she knew what was happening. He was beyond control, and if she could not stop him he would take her here, a perfect stranger making himself master of her body.

Rhys, she thought drowningly. Rhys. And knew that she must bring an end to it without angering him.

As if she dealt with a madman she released her hands from their grip on his shoulders, slid them slowly across the wide taut expanse of skin and muscle and waited until his mouth lifted from its sensuous exploration of her throat before pulling back in his embrace.

He did not prevent her. Like her, he was breathing heavily, his eyelids drooping above the pale glitter of his eyes. As she fought for self-command the mouth that had wreaked such damage firmed slowly into a straight line.

After a moment he dropped his arms, permitting her to step away. Arminel shivered, terrified at the onslaught of desire which had engulfed her. Her skin prickled, but deep in her body she felt the painful ache of passion denied, the bitter pangs of frustration.

'So now,' Kyle said in thick tones, 'what do we do?'

'Nothing!' She turned away as she spoke, pulling her jacket to her with quick, nervous movements.

'Just pretend it never happened?'

She winced at the sardonic inflection in the deep voice, but replied as steadily as she could, 'Yes.'

Forget everything, the sudden remorseless desire which had kindled in them both at that first kiss, the primitive, unreasoning sexuality which had shaken them into each other's arms—forget, too, the wild response he had called forth from her body.

'Well, you may be able to,' he observed with satirical emphasis, 'but I'm damned if I can. You wanted me as much as I wanted you, Arminel.'

'I know, I——' She couldn't go on. Miserably remembering the promise she had given Rhys, she said weakly, 'Oh, can't we just leave it? I—I must have been mad!'

'A fairly common madness.' He had recovered much more quickly than she, for his voice was judicious, coolly detached. 'Most people call it sex. But you recognised it, I'm sure, the minute we set eyes on each other, just as I did.'

'*No!*' She made a swift negatory gesture, hunching her shoulders. 'No, it wasn't—I didn't——'

'Try and convince yourself if you want to.' Now he sounded bored. 'But don't try it on me. I knew as soon as I saw you that you were a hot little wanton. No wonder you gave Rhys such a pleasant holiday! Shall I tell him that you respond equally fervently to any man who kisses you?'

Whirling, hand raised to strike the sneer from his mouth, Arminel was caught and held, the magnificent mask of his face cold with disdain as his fingers tightened to pain on her wrist.

'Don't be silly,' he said, and kissed her again, using his masculine strength to force her into accepting the domination of his mouth.

Arminel gave a convulsive shudder, then concentrated on fighting, not him but herself. For the flame caught her again, running through her brain and her blood until all reality was that burning, searching kiss and her response to it.

'See?' he taunted, releasing her. 'Enjoy your holiday here, Arminel. Just don't go thinking of it as one that will last a lifetime. That way no one will get hurt. And if you don't want to end up in my bed keep out of my way!'

She could not reply. Her mouth opened, but no words would come and she had to turn away from the derisive contempt of his face. One of the dogs pressed himself against her knees; absently she bent and stroked the woolly forehead while brown intelligent eyes blinked up at her. Offering sympathy? Comfort? He was the only one on Te Nawe likely to.

Silently they drove down the other side of the mountain towards an area which was a kind of plateau divided by narrow streams and bounded on two sides by steep hills which fell away to wider valleys, one with Te Nawe homestead in it, the other an area of dairy farms. The third side was cliffs three hundred feet high, so Kyle informed her laconically as they joined the County road, here not in much better shape than the farm track. After a short distance they left it again for the paddocks on the other side of the road, still part of Te Nawe.

'A very important part,' said Kyle, stopping the Land Rover on a long narrow strip of what appeared to be mown grass. 'This is the airstrip. All of Te Nawe is fertilised from here. The building contains the storage bins for the fertiliser. Coming?'

'How far away are the cliffs?'

He looked at her. 'Just across the paddock. Be careful, they go straight down.'

They did, too, and three hundred feet of red rock was a long drop down to the sea that crawled at the base.

Arminel took one look, thankful for the wires which prevented the animals from falling over. Slowly, hands in her pockets, she walked along the fence, admiring the stark efficiency of post and wire. Not beautiful but oh, how efficient! Below and to one side the sea glittered like a promise. In the summer it would lose the bright cold radiance of winter, become a deeper, softer colour. But she would never see it.

A gull wailed plaintively like a lost soul but high above in the bright sky a lark sang, the cascade of sound ecstatic in the cool, bright air.

I'm like the gull, she thought scornfully, a lost soul. For it seemed that her whole conception of herself was wrong. Practical, with plenty of common sense—she had always been rather proud of her common sense. Yet she had behaved like a wanton idiot up there on Te Nawe, throwing her concept of her personality to the winds by acting so wildly out of character. She was afraid and bewildered and shocked by the depths of passion she had discovered in herself. It was like suddenly discovering another person living inside your body. Terrifying. Yet she was not surprised. Somehow, some primitive part of her had immediately recognised that basic magnetism and been afraid of it. When her eyes first rested on Kyle's arrogant face her body had accepted him as a lover, mindlessly, without any conscious awareness of attraction. What she had taken to be dislike was now revealed as the pull of desire, deep-seated, the simple call of woman to man signalling submission and availability.

He had known it. Where her innocence had tried to convince her that the sparks they struck from each other were caused by distrust his wider experience had recognised the chemistry for what it was.

I shall never be so innocent again, Arminel thought wearily, hunching her shoulders against the wind. For until those explosive minutes in Kyle's arms she had always thought that attraction and liking went together.

Now she knew that one could despise and fear someone, yet still feel a hungry rapture at their touch.

It must never happen again, she vowed, turning back to the airstrip. Never again. Because what her subconscious was telling her, however mutedly, was that she could become addicted to the fiery tide of sensation he invoked in her. And he was a hard man; to be at his mercy would be to know misery indeed.

As she walked across the short, damp grass she realised that Kyle was watching her. The dogs lay quietly in the shade of the Land Rover, tails thumping gently as she approached; one snapped at a fly, then looked absurdly disgusted at its failure to catch the insect.

'Have some coffee,' said Kyle as she came up to him. How could he behave as though nothing had happened?

Probably because for him nothing had. No doubt he was accustomed to making love; his experience certainly showed. That sudden uprush of desire would be nothing new to him. No, she was just another nubile, willing woman, she decided savagely as she accepted a mug of coffee from him, and the reason that thought hurt was because—well, because she *wasn't*. Such abandon was totally foreign to her nature.

When they arrived back after a silent trip Davina Rattray was there, ensconced on the verandah with Rhys and Mrs Beringer. And when Kyle greeted her with a kiss it was obvious that although pleasantly fluttered by his masculine attraction, her whole being was bent on Rhys. Not that Rhys seemed to mind. In spite of his declaration that she did nothing to him he treated her with a friendly affection which must have infuriated her.

She was a pretty little thing, with glossy nut-brown curls and enormous dark eyes above a ripe, curving mouth. Her pleasant, deep voice was at odds with her breathless, little-girl looks, and she spoke with the same accent as Mrs Beringer, one obviously taught at girls' boarding schools, because neither of the men produced those rather affected vowel sounds.

Arminel, whose foster-parents had been English with a fussy attitude towards speech, was glad that they had insisted that the children in their care speak well. Still raw from the morning's traumatic events, she was sourly pleased that at least the Beringers couldn't use her accent as a weapon in the war they fought with her.

Davina was charming. Even when she and her hostess and Kyle were discussing a book Arminel had vaguely heard of, and Davina asked, 'What did you think of it, Arminel?' she was sweet.

Even sweeter when Arminel said that she hadn't read it.

'Well, we had to read the classics at school,' Davina said, 'and very boring I found them, too. But this is different, being one of the few I've enjoyed.'

Yes, she was charming, in spite of the fact that between them all they managed to make Arminel aware of the great gaps in her education. Of course she had always intended to do something about the fact that she knew little of her cultural heritage, but somehow the years spent earning a living had got in the way.

Laziness, she told herself, and vowed that when she got back home she would settle down to a steady diet of self-improvement. It was one thing she could salvage from this holiday.

'Of course Australians are very sporting, aren't they?' said Davina, for all the world as though she was discussing the physical characteristics of some rare type of wild animal. 'What sports do you play, Arminel?'

'None with any degree of skill. Just the usual ones; I swim and surf and I play tennis.' Arminel deliberately underplayed her expertise.

'Oh, lovely! Have you seen the tennis court here? And the swimming pool?'

At Arminel's negative answer she said, 'Why, we

must have a game tonight. We could play mixed doubles. Unless Rhys is too tired, of course.'

This was apparently a joke, because Rhys leaned over the table and pulled one of the curls at her temple, growling, 'Watch it, kiddo!'

Davina laughed and Arminel looked up, her eyes unwillingly held by Kyle's. She read there cold satisfaction. You see, he pointed out without words, how suited they are to each other.

And he was right. However reluctant Rhys was to admit it, the sweet ebullient Davina was ideal for him. She would adore him so fervently that he would never again feel the chill of comparison with his brother and together they would glide happily through life.

How strange that Arminel should be so calmly viewing his marriage to another when until yesterday she had been almost sure that she loved him!

She refused to admit to herself why her attitude was so detached.

When afternoon drew on towards evening they played mixed doubles as Davina wanted, she and Rhys against Kyle and Arminel, who defeated them with almost contemptuous ease.

'Well played,' said Rhys, but his expression was sullen as he dropped an arm about Arminel's shoulders. 'That's a powerful backhand you've got there, my sweet.'

He didn't like being beaten. 'I practise it,' Arminel said lightly. 'When life gets too much for me I go out and smash tennis balls into a wall. It's very satisfying.'

He chuckled and bent to whisper in her ear, 'Next time play with me. Davina's almost in the rabbit class!'

Which was unfair, as his own serve had let his partner down rather badly.

Kyle and Davina followed them in. Fancifully Arminel was sure that she could feel two pairs of eyes boring into the back of her head, but the displeasure in Mrs Beringer's eyes was no flash of fancy.

It was an awkward situation. Arminel couldn't prevent herself from feeling sorry for Davina, whose pansy-brown eyes filled with hurt whenever they rested on Rhys, which was most of the time. But she was sympathetic to Rhys, too. His mother was using totally unfair tactics to pressure him into an engagement for which he wasn't yet ready. Surely the older woman could see that if she took a leaf out of Kyle's book and left them strictly alone Rhys would probably come to realise just how much he liked Davina.

They were going entirely the wrong way about things, Davina and Mrs Beringer. Arminel wished rather desperately that she hadn't let herself be talked into this stupid charade. It was distinctly wearing on the nerves, acting the scarlet woman. And if Rhys really felt no more than affection for Davina why couldn't he summon up the strength to tell his mother so and demand that she stop this harassment which must only lead to grief for someone?

When, outside her bedroom door, she asked him this he sighed. 'You wouldn't realise, but it's hard to tell your mother where to get off. She loves me and I don't like to hurt her feelings. I've always been her favourite. Kyle's too self-contained; he was Dad's son. She relies on me for affection. She and Kyle don't have anything in common, but until all this blew up she and I were the best of friends.'

As she opened her lips to protest he kissed her. 'Don't scold me, Arminel, I've had enough.'

Which was all very well, but didn't he realise just how blatantly he was using her as a shield between his mother and himself? No, she thought, he wouldn't. Rhys was not accustomed to questioning his own actions; he was not at all aware of the many excuses the brain could manufacture to hide the less pleasant results of our actions from ourselves.

'I don't like hurting people,' she mumbled, avoiding his questing mouth. 'This—this act of ours is upsetting your mother and hurting Davina. She's a sweet little thing ...'

'Oh, hell, that's what makes it so hard,' he groaned. 'She looks at me with those great big brown eyes and I feel like a heel. But how can I marry her if I don't love her? It's you I want.'

'You promised——'

'I know.' He accepted her quick withdrawal, but his eyes were very bright and challenging as they surveyed her worried face. 'But don't forget that I want you, Arminel, and I'm not giving up, not for Mum, not for Davina, not for big brother. I'm going to keep telling you that until you believe me. And then I'm going to persuade you to love me, too. You did at Surfers, you can here. I know that you hate this situation, you're so frank and open that it must go against the grain, but honestly, if we just jog quietly along everything will work out fine in the end.'

# CHAPTER FIVE

UNFORTUNATELY for Rhys's blithe confidence things didn't happen that way. The following days revealed that Davina's arrival on the scene had hardened Mrs Beringer's attitude towards her other guest. She was never again openly rude to her, but she let no chance slip by to make Arminel feel an outsider.

And for all her sweetness and charm Davina was a woman fighting for her man; Arminel had to admit that it would be expecting superhuman restraint to hope that the girl would not follow her hostess's lead.

Probably life would have been easier if she could dislike the younger girl, but she could not. Each day that went past only increased her conviction that Davina was the perfect girl for Rhys.

Arminel could not rid herself of the suspicion that Rhys was rather enjoying himself flaunting his beautiful girl-friend in the teeth of his mother and his brother. No doubt it was good for his ego to drop a light kiss on her mouth when they met and parted, to let his hand linger on her arm, to sit beside her in the evenings and talk to her in a low, intimate voice.

Several times she had almost made up her mind to leave. It was the only sensible thing to do, to get out and let them fight it out amongst themselves. She told herself that the reason why she stayed was because Rhys was not strong enough to stand up to them all. Sometimes she almost convinced herself that this was so.

But in the night when sleep refused to come she knew who it was who filled her mind with forbidden thoughts and her body with an aching hunger of frustration.

Kyle was busy. In spite of his mother's protests he

spent many of his evenings in his study and the very modern, well-equipped office next door to it. During the time he was with the family he flirted lightly with Davina, viewed his brother with a grim mockery which should have made Rhys exceedingly uneasy, and allowed no emotion to show in his eyes and voice when he spoke to Arminel.

But always between them was an awareness, spine-tingling, unseen as electricity yet more potent than a high tension current. He rarely touched her, but wherever his eyes rested, on her mouth, on the tiny betrayal in her throat, on the gentle curves of her breast, there was a sudden warmth as though he caressed her there. Every pulse in her body came painfully alive and she had to stop herself from dreaming erotic, impossible dreams. While she was awake she remained in control of her brain, but in sleep the subconscious is free, and often she woke, shocked, at the explicit nature of her dreams, her body tormented by instincts and needs she had never before experienced.

When Kyle was near she was nervous and wary. She managed to avoid watching him, but her skin acted as her eyes, telling her exactly where he was in the room.

He knew, of course. Or rather, he too was subjected to this acute physical desire. He made a better job of hiding it, but she often felt the impact of his eyes on her and the tension which throbbed between them was so tangible that she wondered why the others couldn't see it.

It was not so bad during the days. They were filled with activity. The homestead needed care, there were expeditions over the station and down to the long ocean beach. Plenty of people visited Te Nawe and they led the busy social life of any country district.

The weather was capricious, but as the weeks went by and the glorious flowers on the magnolias were replaced by the ardent green of the new leaves the lengthening days grew warmer. In the orchard behind the house apple trees displayed their red-tipped blossom to the sky and citrus began to bloom, the sweet perfume floating on the quiet air.

One day Arminel wandered beneath the peach trees accompanied by Smitty the cat. Mrs Beringer and Davina had gone to play golf and she was revelling in her solitude. Never before had she been so hemmed in by people; in spite of the size of the homestead she was beginning to feel claustrophobic.

She was alien to Te Nawe and its owners. That fact was only too obvious. Even Rhys sometimes seemed astonished at her lack of knowledge of the things they discussed. Like most proud people Arminel hated being forced on to the defensive. But the values she had were not theirs; it seemed strange to her that Davina should find a job totally irrelevant to her way of life, whereas the skills that Arminel was proud of, her efficiency, her ability to run an office, were worth nothing to them.

The sound of her name was an intrusion. Frowning, she turned, slitting her eyes against the sunlight. Rhys had said nothing—but no, this wasn't Rhys.

At Kyle's approach she stopped beside a big grapefruit tree studded with large golden globes of fruit and waited, her expression wary.

'Come on,' he said smoothly.

'Where?'

'I'm going to give you your first riding lesson.'

Her teeth clamped momentarily on to her bottom lip. 'I—well, I'm not——'

'Oh, stop dithering,' he said impatiently. Reaching out a hand, he took hers and began to walk off between the rows of trees, dragging her with him as though she weighed nothing.

His hand was warm and strong and merciless. For an instant Arminel pulled back, but a jerk that almost hauled her off her feet changed her mind about resisting. Or perhaps it was the excitement that submerged common sense to the flaring hunger which licked through her body at his touch.

Beyond the fence two horses waited. Arminel knew nothing at all about horses, but she had a good, although untutored eye for form and balance and beauty and she realised that these two were a cut above the usual station hacks. Several cuts above, in fact.

The smaller one was a mare, glossy as a ripe chestnut with a white flash above a pair of mildly enquiring eyes. As they came up to her she twitched her ears forward and snuffled gently down her nostrils.

'This,' Kyle said casually, 'is Tessa. As well as being beautiful she's placid and gentle, so there's no need for that hunted look.'

It was not Tessa who caused that hunted look and he knew it, but Arminel followed his lead even while she wondered just why he had sought her out. It was almost an act of foolhardiness.

'She looks valuable,' she said apprehensively, trying to clear her mind of all but the prospect of riding.

Kyle lifted an eyebrow. 'She is valuable. Why?'

'Can't you hurt their mouths, or something? I don't want to ruin her, or hurt her.'

There was a quiet creak from the hinges of the gate as he pushed it open. The sun blazed suddenly blue in Arminel's hair. The suffocating intensity of her emotions almost drowned her; without realising what she was doing she lifted her head and looked at him, her eyes so dark that all blueness had fled from them.

For a long moment they stared at each other, Arminel searching his face in a desperate attempt to find something more than dislike and desire there.

Roughly he turned her towards the horses, not attempting to moderate the strength in his fingers.

'If you're heavy-handed I'll let you know,' he said with harsh distinctness. 'Let's go.'

It was as sharp a rebuff as a slap in the face, but it had the effect of bracing her. She *would not* beg—for anything! Especially not for gentleness and understanding which he did not possess.

Surprisingly he was an excellent teacher, extremely patient and careful, quick to praise and never losing sight of the fact that she knew not even the most rudimentary thing about riding.

Under his tutelage and with Tessa's co-operation, she learned how to mount and dismount, the correct grip for the reins and how to adjust the girth and stirrups.

'Yes,' he said coolly, watching as she walked the willing Tessa around in a circle. 'You have excellent hands. I thought you would. That's enough for today. You can come with me down to the paddock and I'll show you how to take the bridle and saddle off.'

Both were silent as they rode past the homestead. Even at the paddock conversation was held to strictly practical subjects.

But when at last Tessa was released with a last affectionate stroke on her soft muzzle Kyle asked, 'Do you want to come into the village with me?'

Arminel's first instinctive shake of her head caused a lifted eyebrow.

'Why not?'

'I don't—well, there's nothing for me to do there.' It was a clumsy answer, but how could she say that the thought of sitting beside him for the half hour or so it took to get to the village was totally intimidating?

'Don't be silly,' he said coolly, taking her arm to turn her back towards the house. 'I've never yet met a woman who didn't like shopping.'

Obviously he had no intention of accepting an excuse. Rather desperately she said, 'But Rhys——'

His fingers tightened on her arm before he released her 'But Rhys——?'

Her tongue tied itself into knots. 'He said he'd take me,' she finally said, lying.

'Ah, but we all know that you'd rather go with me.'

This was said with such bland assurance that for a moment the meaning didn't register. When it did she stumbled, her feet symbolising the shock his words caused.

'Well?' Kyle asked softly.

She shook her head, not daring to look at him in case he saw the confirmation of his remark in her face.

He laughed. 'As it happens, you can do something for me. I have a young cousin who must be about your age and I want to get her a birthday present. Mama's ideas run to the conventional, but Katie is a very modern young woman.'

'So you want *me* to choose?'

'Is that so surprising?' His voice was smooth as cream. 'You have natural good taste, as I'm sure you know. Your clothes are very carefully chosen to emphasise your attractions.'

It was a compliment, two compliments in fact, so why did she feel as though he had slapped her in the face?

'Thank you,' she said with stiff politeness.

He chuckled, infuriatingly, and mocked, 'Hard to please, aren't you? I don't go in for flattery, Arminel.'

No, and he didn't go in for pleasing, either, he was too arrogantly confident to worry about buttering anyone up. So why, when she was so suspicious, did she find herself meekly agreeing to go with him?

'Because,' she told her reflection in the mirror, 'you are an idiot.'

It seemed as good a reason as any. As well as the overmastering physical pull that basic antagonism was still there, even though he hid it under this new relaxed attitude. Probably he had assessed the situation between her and Rhys and what he saw had caused him to subdue his hostility. He wouldn't have to be very astute to wonder why, if she was in love with his brother, she had responded with such ardour to the pass he had made up on Te Nawe.

And he was an extremely clever man, worldly and knowledgeable with a brain like iced quicksilver. She was afraid of him, and not only because she hungered for his lovemaking with every fibre in her being. Davina might call him a darling, but some instinct in Arminel saw deeper to the tough uncompromising core of his character. He would be as unsparing and as exacting with himself as with others; a man to fear.

She ran her suddenly damp hand down the seam of her tailored shirt jacket, aware that the sand colour repeated and emphasised the apricot of her slacks. Her fingers trembled as she tugged a little fretfully at the collar of the cream blouse she wore. Davina dressed exquisitely in silks and fine wools and linens, expensive materials crafted by famous names. Typists couldn't afford such clothes, but within her budget she did rather well, Arminel decided.

The village was a small collection of shops and houses beside a little harbour. In bad weather boats clogged the wharf and during the summer visitors flocked to the beaches. It was a busy, cheerful place, centre for a large, wealthy farming district, so the shops were good.

'Just prowl,' Kyle told her laconically as he got out of the car. 'You're bound to see something. I'll be an hour or so.'

'Where——'

He grinned. 'The dentist.'

'Oh, poor you!' For the first time ever in his presence her laughter was clear and untrammelled, although her sympathy was warmly evident.

'I don't know why everyone thinks it's so funny,' he complained, his eyes roving her face. 'I'm terrified!'

'You look it.' But she composed her expression into one of more seemly gravity. 'Good luck.'

'Why, thank you, ma'am.' He bowed, did it superbly too, then walked away from her down the street, as beautiful in his own way as his horses were, a delight to the eye.

Arminel turned, pretending to stare into a window, but her eyes followed his reflection, noting the smooth grace of his stride, the lean, powerful body held with the controlled confidence of a superbly fit animal.

People looked at him, most smiled and received smiles back. A cold pang of envy tore into Arminel's heart. She would give anything to be a friend to him. But even as the thought entered her mind she rejected it. No, she had something of him which none of these kindly people possessed. Dislike her as much as he did, whenever he looked at her he wanted her, and she would not exchange that for all the friendship in the world. It hurt that there had been other women who had aroused him; she knew that there would be others in the future. But at the moment she was the one, the focus of his attention. And there was nothing his cold, clever brain could do about it.

Watching him, she felt something expand within her and suddenly the day was glittering, as filled with colour and glamour as a soap bubble.

Twenty minutes later Kyle found her in a gift shop, touching with tender fingers a burnished green and copper pottery bowl.

From then on the day became like something out of time. He teased her and made her laugh, insisted on buying her lunch in the town's one and only restaurant, and though it was a little public, as everyone knew him and came up to pay their respects, it was exciting, too, for between them the awareness glittered and spun, an almost tangible tension, exquisitely thrilling.

They argued amicably over a gift for his cousin before finally agreeing on a cobwebby shawl in the palest smoky-mauve, spun and knitted by a local woman.

'But is it fashionable?' Kyle objected.

'It doesn't need to be fashionable.' Arminel touched it gently. 'It's beautiful.'

His glance lanced through her as though he was trying to see into her soul. Faint colour touched the high, beautiful curve of her cheekbones.

'O.K.,' he said with an abruptness which sparred uneasily with his relaxed mood of a moment ago. 'May I quote you on that?'

She smiled as she was meant to, but said uneasily, 'You know her, Kyle. If you don't think——'

'My dear, I'm sure your taste is impeccable.' He turned and the woman of the shop came up eagerly at the subtle summons. 'We'll take this,' he told her, all charm.

'It's beautiful, isn't it?' She was curious about his companion, but only a quick look revealed it.

When the parcel had been wrapped she said, 'Thank you, Kyle; I'll tell Mary Hobday that you liked it.'

Once out in the car he said, 'Now, tell me the meaning of that rather peculiar look you gave me.'

Before she could reconsider Arminel said, 'Oh, just— well, I've never shopped with anyone whose approval would make a craftsman as happy as she thought Mary Hobday was going to be. Kyle Beringer, patron of the arts and an occasional craft.'

'That was a rather cynical remark,' he said, apparently amused as he set the car in motion.

'It wasn't meant to be.' Some tinge of the chagrin she felt when they discussed things she had no knowledge of made her say wryly, 'I'm out of my depth, I suppose.'

'But fast learning to swim.'

From the village the road climbed a steep hill; it had been several days since the last rain and behind them dust collected in a great cloud, but the big car was so well engineered that not even a faint taste of it touched her lips.

'No answer?' Kyle asked lightly.

She shook her head. 'There is no answer to that.'

'Then tell me whether you like Davina.'

After a moment's hesitation she said, 'I doubt if anyone could dislike her. To use her own words, she's a darling.'

'Yet you don't mind hurting her?'

His voice was almost remote as though he was speaking of cold abstractions, not a woman's heart.

Wretchedly Arminel drew a deep breath. 'I—yes, of course I hate hurting her.'

'You're just not prepared to do anything about it.'

She stared down at her hands in her lap, concentrating fiercely on keeping them still. It hurt to find herself flung back into warfare and she found herself wondering miserably if he had used his considerable charm to soften her up for this confrontation. She cursed herself for being so stupid and she hated Kyle for being ruthless enough to force the issue just now, when she had been so happy.

'I can't—Kyle, it's not fair to try to push Rhys into something he doesn't want! It's not fair to him and it's certainly not fair to Davina.'

'If he really didn't want it there would be no hope of pushing him into anything,' he said implacably. 'He's weak, but not that weak.'

'But if he was persuaded into marrying her how long do you think it would last?'

'As long as any other, longer than most.'

He should have needed to keep all his concentration on the narrow, winding road. On one side the sun shone in tiger-stripes through a row of huge macrocarpa trees, dazzling the eyes and making it hard driving.

But Kyle continued his attack. 'With you out of the way he'd very soon realise that he's been in love with Davina for years. You have the novelty of a willing disposition and provocative beauty, but as you pointed out a few minutes ago, you don't belong. And Davina does.'

Deep inside her heart something snapped. Words would not come. She stared down at her hands, trying to tell him—what? Nothing. There was nothing she could say in her own defence. The past couple of weeks had convinced her that Kyle was right, that Rhys loved Davina without realising it, but she could not—would not say so. Kyle didn't care how much he hurt her, his whole sympathy was for Davina, who belonged.

At last she said in a tight voice, 'Time will tell.'

'Time? How about money?' And when she didn't say

anything he continued calmly, 'How much, Arminel? What would it be worth to you to pack up and go, leaving the field open for Davina?'

The insult left her quite literally breathless. When she could breathe it was to an intolerable stabbing pain and she looked, horrified and shaken, down at hands that had formed themselves into claws.

'Nothing,' she said with the cold despair of hopelessness, 'nothing that you could give me will persuade me to go.'

'He won't marry you,' he said, almost casually.

'Then why are you so eager to get rid of me?'

'So you do think you might pull off a marriage.' He ran the car into a layby, a curve which had once been the road but was now cut off by a new line of survey.

It was overhung by a woodlot of tall, thin, carefully pruned pines. Closer to the road was a small forest of tree-ferns, their rough black trunks a harsh contrast to the silver reverses of the huge scrolled leaves.

Kyle said cruelly, 'You'll never do it. When it comes to the crunch Rhys won't stand up for you however good you are in bed. He wants a wife he can be proud of, not one he'd have to apologise for.'

The colour had fled from her face, leaving it chiselled into cold pride, the only colour the pink curves of her mouth and the deep navy-blue of her eyes.

'That's my business,' she said, and by some act of kindness from a gentle genie, her voice was as level and steady as his.

'And mine,' he said, watching her from beneath partly lowered eyelids. He smiled suddenly and reached out to trace the outline of her lips. They trembled beneath his fingertip. 'Be sensible,' he said, his tones deepening. 'I don't blame you for using your face and that delectable body to improve your prospects, but one thing adventurers should learn is when to cut their losses. Rhys is a loss. You don't love him and what he feels for you is infinitely more basic than love. It's

Davina he feels protective towards, Davina he jokes with and teases and talks to, not you.'

'I hate you!' she choked, twisting her face away from the soft torture of his finger on her mouth.

'Because the fact that you want me gets in the way of all your plans?' he taunted.

As she watched, fascinated and unable to move, the pale blaze of his eyes darkened. Releasing his seatbelt, he leaned towards her, not stopping until his mouth was resting as light as a feather's kiss on hers.

'Because you do, don't you, Arminel?' he said, very low, and kissed her, his mouth moving sensuously over hers as if she was the one person his body and mind craved. Arminel jerked away, but he followed her down, forcing her head back into the headrest while he openly demonstrated just how much power he possessed over her.

For only their mouths touched. He did not have to hold her. Yet she could not move, or do anything but respond with all the fiery abandon he had woken to life in her.

When at last he lifted his mouth he looked down into her face with cold hostility.

'I want you out,' he said, each word icily distinct. 'You've caused enough havoc. Make your excuses tonight and get out tomorrow. Or I'll use the other weapon I've got.' His finger flicked her mouth, slightly swollen in the pallor of her face. 'And I'll enjoy that,' he said, and it was a threat.

Not another word was exchanged until they got home. Then he said, 'Remember, Arminel.'

What she might have answered was never said. Probably it was just as well. Arminel was so confused, so racked by anger and a kind of sick, cold desolation, that she might have lost her head completely.

But at that exact moment Mrs Beringer and Davina arrived home, so she was forced to appear as normal as possible. Both possessed a sharp pair of eyes, both watched her constantly even when Rhys was nowhere in sight.

When at last she made it to her bedroom the solitude she thought she craved was intolerable. She did not want to have to face Kyle's betrayal just yet. Betrayal? A bitter smile made her expression suddenly cynical. He at least knew exactly what he felt for her. He had made no attempt to pretty up that basic lust with emotions he didn't feel. And now he had delivered the ultimatum she had been subconsciously dreading ever since she had arrived at Te Nawe.

The bright sensuous room mocked her anger and self-contempt. She pulled on a pair of jeans and a jersey and went out across the lawn and down through the drifting petals of the flowering cherries to the farthest part of the garden, a glade beneath the unfamiliar trees of the New Zealand bush, darkly foliaged, lush, with three silver ferns rising in spiral symmetry towards the sky.

She dropped on to the rustic seat beneath a tree with small chocolate flowers so heavily perfumed that they tormented her nostrils, the sensual scent contrasting piquantly with the cool fresh evening air.

For a long time her head drooped as she stared unseeingly at the smooth grass between her feet. Her thoughts were inchoate, painful with forbidden hungers, needs which only her will-power prevented from overwhelming her. So she was half in love with Kyle—no, she fancied him like mad. Love was too fine a word to dignify the way he affected her. She wanted him. Just that, no more. He was too hard, too self-sufficient, too calculating to love. Physically he was all that a man could be, possessed of a rare sexual tension which made him intensely attractive.

During a self-indulgent moment or two she allowed her mind to fantasise before grimacing and dragging it back on to proper paths. Just because he was tall and lean and bronze-skinned, just because he had features which formed a hard mask of perfection, just because his eyes made it only too obvious that when he looked at her he wanted to take what he saw—these were potent weapons in his armoury, but she must fight them. For he had the power to strip every vestige of self-respect from her, and he knew it. If she gave him the opportunity he would take her, carelessly, with superb skill, and then discard her just as carelessly. And that could break her.

For the first time she admitted that her defences were so fragile that he would have little difficulty in breaching them.

He knew that, too. In the car he had delivered his ultimatum with imperious confidence, very sure of his ability to enforce it. The cool inflexible voice had made it quite clear that if she didn't leave he had every intention of making love to her with a ruthless passion that frightened her—and yes, it must be admitted—excited her too.

'I must be mad,' she said beneath her breath, but she knew her skin had heated at the thought of discovering just how good a lover he was. Pictures slid into her mind, and she bit her lip, banishing them with a fist pressed into her mouth. Above it her eyes were desperate, large and glittering as though she suffered a fever.

That was all that it was, of course. A fever in the blood, but it ached through her body, drawing her breath in short shallow panting movements, until she said again, 'I must be mad,' and jumped to her feet, running back through the quiet afternoon as though she had seen a dark angel beneath the silver ferns.

# CHAPTER SIX

WHEN Arminel came along past the office it was to hear the sound of raised voices through a door not quite closed. Kyle. Kyle and Rhys. For a moment she hesitated, frowning, her ears straining to hear. Then she sighed and made her way past. She would only make matters worse.

Davina was waiting, a Davina tight-lipped and, in spite of her excellent make-up, bearing signs of a bout of weeping. They exchanged wary smiles and Davina said something innocuous about the weather.

Following her lead, Arminel found herself thinking that in another situation she and Davina could have been friends. Or if not friends at least friendly acquaintances. But then in any other situation she and Davina would not have met.

Mrs Beringer was next, her expression so composed that for a moment Arminel thought she knew nothing of her sons' quarrel. Until she met the full impact of the older woman's gaze and read bitter condemnation there. Arminel checked a sigh. Much as she hated to give in to Kyle's threats, it was obvious that her time here was over. She would tell Rhys tomorrow. Misplaced notions of loyalty could not be allowed to cover the fact that her presence was an irritant. Life at Te Nawe would be much simpler for everyone when she left.

When Rhys arrived he was in a strange mood. At first it seemed that the quarrel had had no effect on his temper, but as the evening wore on it was clear that beneath his lighthearted attitude there was another, darker mood. He treated Davina to a half-aggressive teasing which revealed only too clearly what had caused her reddened eyelids, ignoring both the protest in his mother's eyes and his brother's icy contempt. Towards Arminel he was almost amorous, sliding quick meaning glances at her, smiling, using every pretence to touch her lightly but possessively. When shortly after dinner Kyle left them Arminel hoped Rhys would stop his calculated provocation. But no, he sat on the arm of her chair and ran his fingers over the slender bones of her shoulder while he pretended to watch television. In a muted voice he whispered compliments, dropped kisses on to her hair and the top of her ear, only leaving her to refill his glass. Quite clearly he and Davina had quarrelled and then there had been the clash with Kyle. Rhys was busy showing both of them that they had no power over him or his actions. In many ways he was very like a child misbehaving when it knows it cannot be reprimanded.

Although Arminel was angry with him she could feel his confusion and pain and her pity made her gentle. If she repudiated him now he would lose face. But compassion would not prevent her from going. Tomorrow she would tell him and he would have to find his own way out of his predicament.

Out on the seat beneath the ponga trees she had at last faced the fact that she had only stayed this long because of Kyle. Now pride impelled her decision. Humiliation was her need to be close to a man who felt nothing for her but a degrading desire laced with contempt.

At last Davina left them, excusing her pallor with the pretext of a headache. Her smile was brave and gallant. Arminel felt her pain as if it was her own. Sickened and angry, she followed her lead.

'Oh, but darling——' Rhys protested, the false affection abruptly banished.

Arminel gave him a steady look, not scornful, but with a measure of reproof.

'I'm tired,' she said quietly.

'Then I'll escort you to your door.'

'You needn't bother.'

But with the obstinacy of the half-intoxicated he came and followed her into her room, ignoring her protests to sit heavily down on the bed. The covers had been turned back; he stared around angrily before he muttered:

'Oh, God, what am I going to do?'

Arminel said nothing.

'We should have got married in Australia,' he pursued, his voice heavy and slurred.

'Even though you're in love with Davina?'

He frowned, then gave her a sly look from beneath his lashes. 'Oh, sit down, for God's sake, Arminel. And don't look at me as though—as though I'm the lowest form of life!' His fingers tugged at the soft sheet. 'Would you let yourself be goaded and chivvied into marriage? Like dogs working sheep, a bark here and there, a little eye-work, always pressure, pressure . . .' His voice trailed away as he watched his fingers plucking aimlessly at the sheet. 'Like a sheep being penned,' he said vaguely, adding with a burst of aggression, 'Nobody sh—should do that to a man. It's—it's not bloody fair!'

'No,' she agreed gently, and came over and sat down beside him, her expression almost loving. He was hurting and he was drunk, and she felt so sorry for him that her heart almost burst, but she had to get him out of here before Kyle found him and took the steps he'd threatened. She shivered, remembering the merciless hardness of his features as he had told her what he would do.

'You must go,' she said. 'You can decide what to do in the morning. You can't stay here, Rhys.'

He smiled vaguely, then lay back against the pillows and went to sleep in spite of everything she could do to stop him.

'Damn!' she muttered when it was quite obvious that

she was getting nowhere. She got up and went across and locked the door. Then she sat down in the chair and waited.

Two hours later he woke, groaning, rubbing his hand across his eyes before he stared around in confusion.

'Lord, I've got a head,' he said fretfully when he saw her.

She nodded and came across to the bed. 'Do you want something for it?'

'Yes.'

He swallowed the aspirin and drank the glass of water she brought him before frowning. 'I'm sorry—I should never drink. Alcohol has that effect on me. And I've not been sleeping very well.'

'It's all right,' she told him, smiling slightly. 'But you'd better go now.'

'Hell, yes.' He sat up, winced, but managed a smile in return. 'You're a darling, Arminel. Sorry I dropped you into this.'

And that was all the apology she would get. He had no idea what he had done to her, what danger he had exposed her to; Rhys was essentially self-centred. Aren't we all? she thought cynically as she unlocked the door for him.

'Thank you,' he said, and kissed her. 'Thanks for everything.'

It was a tacit farewell and she accepted it as such, laughing. 'You're welcome. Now for heaven's sake go before someone sees you.'

'Oh, that's all I need,' he agreed morosely.

While he was asleep she had cleaned off all her make-up. Now she undressed and pulled on her nightgown, then got into bed, lying on her back with her hands behind her head, staring up into the darkness. Outside some small night insect shirr-shirred to itself. Through the open french window floated the scent of clove carnations. Frogs called, kraak-kraak, and she found herself wondering how they organised it so that they all croaked in concert, like a well-drilled choir. It was one of those languorous spring nights when everything seems awake and expectant.

There was no sound from next door. Not that there ever was. The homestead was well built and in spite of his size Kyle moved with a noiselessness which reminded her of a big jungle cat.

Kyle. Her mouth dried as she pretended that she had the daring of the truly desperate. Like her, he slept with his french windows opened to the sweet night air. If she had the courage enough nothing could be easier than to slip across the terrace and into his room. She had never been in there, but the starshine was bright enough for her to see and she would just stand inside the door, listening for his breathing. Like a wraith, silent, unseen, she would make her way across to his bed and slide free of her nightdress before she slipped between the sheets to join him.

And what would happen then? Contemptuous rejection, or equally contemptuous possession? She did not know, and although her body was singing with desire, she was not about to find out. Each was equally humiliating, each would mark her for life.

She half turned, suppressing a sob, and jerked upright as the door opened. Not Rhys again, surely!

'Who—who is it?'

'Don't tell me you weren't expecting me.'

No—not Rhys.

'What—what do you want?'

Teeth gleamed in the hard mask of his face as his eyes flashed over her shoulders and the long bare arm clutching the sheet to her as she sat up. He switched on a wall lamp as he came towards the bed. In its light he was enormous, a dark, dangerous man, such menace in his expression that her heart stopped in her throat.

'Kyle?' she whispered.

'I warned you,' he said silkily. 'I never say what I don't mean. Did you really think you could get away

with it? You shouldn't have made such a public
farewell, darling. I have uncommonly good hearing.'

Twice she tried to order him out, but the words
couldn't force their way past the tension in her throat.
His smoky gaze burned as it fixed on the muscles
working fruitlessly beneath the silken skin.

'I'd been along to his room to make my peace with
him,' he said between his teeth. 'So I had a pretty good
idea where he was. Did you decide to risk everything on
a last throw, darling? It won't work, you know. You're
leaving tomorrow, but at least you'll be able to compare
techniques. His and mine.'

'No!' she gasped, warding him off with her hands.

'Yes.' His eyes lanced up to meet hers and she winced
at the hatred she saw in them. He spoke rapidly,
thickly, the words underlined with a concentrated
contempt which seared her. 'Why protest? It's what
you've wanted ever since you arrived here. I knew
within five minutes of laying eyes on you that I could
have you any time I wanted. Tramps like you are easy
enough to understand.'

Arminel's eyes fell to the hands resting on his hips.
They were trembling as if he resisted an unbearable
urge to hurt her.

'Yes,' he said harshly as she closed her eyes and shook
her head, half in terror, half in anger, 'you've turned this
house into a hell-hole. How do you do it? How can a slut
like you create such turmoil and desperation and pain?
What is it that promises me such untold, unknowable
delights when I look at you, incites me, excites me until I
can't think of anything else but my need to know how you
feel and sound and taste when I make love to you?'

He smiled with cruel purpose and stretched out his
hand. Repelled and angered though she was by the grim
savagery of his words, they struck home in some deep
primitive part of her, and she felt her breath come faster
through her lips. But she twisted away, trying to fling
herself across the bed and out of reach. Kyle laughed

softly beneath his breath, a chilling sound on the waiting air, and caught a handful of hair.

'Tonight,' he said, ignoring the tears which started to her eyes. 'I'm going to find out if that promise is genuine or as worthless as the rest of you, you tormenting, teasing . . .'

Her hands tugged against his, trying to free her maltreated scalp. He cursed and wrenched the sheet back and came down beside her twisting, writhing body, its pale slenderness barely hidden by the drift of blue lawn that was her nightdress.

'Pretty,' he said, almost calmly. 'Take it off.'

'*No!*' she spat, her expression fierce as she jerked her knee upwards, hoping to catch him where it hurt.

He was ready for her. With contemptuous ease he bundled her over on to her face, then while she gasped into the pillow and fought for breath he grabbed her flailing wrists and held them up behind her shoulders at an angle just the wrong side of pain. One knee held her legs pressed into the mattress.

Arminel turned her head sideways, half sobbing with fear and outrage. The smooth material of the pillowslip and the sheet moved sensuously against her cheek and throat.

'Kyle——' she began, hating herself for pleading. 'It wasn't what you think. Nothing happened. You must believe me——'

'I'll believe that to you nothing happened.' His voice was level, almost bored. 'I don't suppose sleeping with Rhys counts as much for you. Ever slept with two brothers in the same night before? Perhaps that will be something for you to remember!'

His mouth brushed her shoulder, moving across the smooth skin in a slow exploration. She could feel the heat of his lips, the small trail of moisture left by his tongue. He was tasting her with open, erotic enjoyment, and her whole body responded in a spasm of hunger and need. His fingers tightened on her wrists.

'Please don't,' she whispered tightly. 'I'm going tomorrow.'

'I know. But before you go we'll get to know each other.'

It was no threat. It was a simple statement of fact. Arminel's skin tightened, grew damp. His mouth moved on its inexorable trail to the nape of her neck; she gasped as he bit gently. 'I don't want to,' she said, her voice high and frightened as that merciless mouth moved with erotic mastery across her shoulders. 'I don't want you.'

'Liar!' He laughed, a soft breathy sound, hot against her sensitised skin. 'I know exactly what you want, because it's what I want too.'

He relaxed his grip on her wrists, but only so that he could hold them both in one hand. His free hand slid beneath the folds of her nightdress, smoothed up her thigh and across her stomach, stopping at her navel to explore. Arminel's whole body jerked; she had never been touched so intimately before, and she was terrified.

'No!' she pleaded thickly. 'Kyle, I don't want this. I've never slept with anyone before and I don't—I can't—please, *don't*!'

'Why do you keep on lying? Does it hurt to tell the truth?' The slurred sensual note in his voice intensified as his hand probed further to cup the curve of her breast. Her sobbing gasp made him laugh again. When his thumb brushed across the tight, unbearably sensitive nub he said derisively, 'Your body doesn't lie, sweetheart.'

Then, so quickly that she could not resist, he dragged her over to face him, the same swift, rough movement serving to haul her nightdress above her head so that her arms were entangled in its folds. Her eyes glared like hot sapphires, her mouth tightened to hide its trembling, but he wasn't even looking at her face. The pale eyes blazed across her breasts, branding her with shame and pain, lingered on the flat plain of her stomach before probing the most intimate parts of her body.

'So you can blush,' he observed sardonically as his head swooped and he took her nipple into his mouth.

A sudden, fierce rigor shook Arminel's body; for a moment she lay taut in his arms as she fought for breath and the strength to resist the ravishing sensations his mouth brought into being from every nerve-end. Beneath her the sheet was warm against her back; she gave a funny, half-choked moan when his mouth traced the contours of each breast. His lips on her skin were torment, torture; she groaned, squeezing her eyes tightly shut, clenching her hands, as his mouth moved to her waist, dropping kisses in a girdle across its narrowness.

She could not move, every muscle locked in a rigid rejection of his practised seduction. When he lifted his head she opened her anguished eyes to stare into his set face. He was frowning slightly, the pale irises swallowed by darkness as he looked down into her flushed agonised countenance. Not even her most stringent efforts could control the soft shaking mouth, the flickering, drooping lashes, the heat along her cheeks as she turned her head away in despair.

He smiled, and lowered his mouth to hers, pushing her head back into the pillow as he explored the soft inner depths. Arched in his arms, she gave in to the promptings of her heart and body, passion overriding her brain in a red haze. He knew, of course. Again there came that set, humourless smile as he pulled her nightdress free, throwing it on to the floor.

She watched as he undressed, her gaze wide, almost distraught as she took in the splendid breadth of shoulders, the play of skin over muscle, the tangle of hair across his chest which arrowed down his stomach. Until then she had not known what physical attraction meant; what had happened before was a pale foreshadowing of this intolerable hunger that racked her now.

His hard warmth against her was the most potent aphrodisiac in the world. Without a word she turned to him, offering him herself. Lost in the sensuous ambience he created for her with his mouth and his hands and his potent masculinity, she followed where he led, barely hearing the words his urgent, harsh voice whispered, her whole being shuddering with sensation until finally, after pain, she entered a delight such as she had never imagined even in her most abandoned fantasies.

Kyle's arms were rigid with corded muscle, separating her from the softness of the pillow. Head flung back, her breath rasping through her lungs, the beat of her heart so strong that she could hear nothing else, Arminel lay at last quiescent beneath a weight at once strange and familiar, her arms locked about his shoulders. Beneath his sweat-soaked skin the muscles that had been rock-hard had lost their tension; like her, he was exhausted, tumbling back through long, slow aeons to reality.

So that's how it is, she thought almost sorrowfully. That is what separates a virgin from the rest of womankind. Not for every woman such a perfect introduction to sexuality, passion combined with a strange tenderness, his knowledge and her innocence melding into an experience of such profound rapture that she thought she could die having known the sweetest that life could offer. Did he know now that she had been a virgin? His experience had been so apparent that she was sure he must.

But she didn't care. The warm expectancy of the night had given way to a drowsy repletion. Tomorrow was far away; tonight was a time out of time.

At last he moved, freeing her. Across the pillow her hair lay in a black sweep of silk; his cheek came to rest on it and he said harshly above her head, 'I've dreamed

## Say Hello to Yesterday
Holly Weston had done it all alone.

She had raised her small son and worked her way up to features writer for a major newspaper. Still the bitterness of the the past seven years lingered.

She had been very young when she married Nick Falconer—but old enough to lose her heart completely when he left. Despite her success in her new life, her old one haunted her.

But it was over and done with—until an assignment in Greece brought her face to face with Nick, and all she was trying to forget. . . .

## Time of the Temptress
The game must be played his way!

Rebellion against a cushioned, controlled life had landed Eve Tarrant in Africa. Now only the tough mercenary Wade O'Mara stood between her and possible death in the wild, revolution-torn jungle.

But the real danger was Wade himself—he had made Eve aware of herself as a woman.

"I saved your neck, so you feel you owe me something," Wade said. "But you don't owe me a thing, Eve. Get away from me." She knew she could make him lose his head if she tried. But that wouldn't solve anything. . . .

## Your Romantic Adventure Starts Here.

## Born Out of Love
It had to be coincidence!

Charlotte stared at the man through a mist of confusion. It was Logan. An older Logan, of course, but unmistakably the man who had ravaged her emotions and then abandoned her all those years ago.

She ought to feel angry. She ought to feel resentful and cheated. Instead, she was apprehensive—terrified at the complications he could create.

"We are not through, Charlotte," he told her flatly. "I sometimes think we haven't even begun."

## Man's World
Kate was finished with love for good.

Kate's new boss, features editor Eliot Holman, might have devastating charms—but Kate couldn't care less, even if it was obvious that he was interested in her.

Everyone, including Eliot, though Kate was grieving over the loss of her husband, Toby. She kept it a carefully guarded secret just how cruelly Toby had treated her and how terrified she was of trusting men again.

But Eliot refused to leave her alone, which only served to infuriate her. He was no different from any other man. . . or was he?

**EXTRA BONUS**
MAIL YOUR ORDER
TODAY AND GET A
FREE TOTE BAG
FROM HARLEQUIN.

that some night your hair was going to make a silk sheet for me. Witch-woman, with your siren's body and your enchantress's face, you could coax me into hell with the fierce delight of your body.'

The slow words sent her pulses throbbing. No longer shy she lifted her hand and traced a path across his chest, touching, stroking, her forefinger deliberately provocative.

'What do you want?' he whispered.

'I want you.' She had said it and she was not going to regret it.

'Show me.'

So she showed him, and told him, her voice throaty and slurred as she indulged her imagination with a hidden desperation. Tonight would be all that she would have of him.

Her whispered love-words hung on the throbbing air until he cut them off with his deep kisses. Then, made wanton by her needs and his desire, she explored him as he had her, shaping him, discovering him by taste and touch and scent, every sense she possessed. At last he groaned in anguish and they came together again in an ecstasy of sensation that left her without thought, without the ability to move.

'Now sleep,' he murmured, and they slept locked together like the ancient Chinese symbol of Yin and Yang, the male and female principles joined to make a perfect whole.

When the night was darkest she woke again to the sound of his voice as he whispered in her ear. It was no startled awakening. Before her mind had assimilated his presence her body had known, responding with a surge of fire to the hand that caressed her slim nakedness.

Wordlessly she turned to him, burying her face in his throat, her open mouth tasting the faint film of salt on his warm smooth skin.

'Circe,' he muttered, his voice heavy with desire and something else, a dark emotion she refused to recognise.

'What kind of spell do you use to enslave a man? Do you sing incantations under the moon to sap will-power and rot strength until honour is gone? I hate you and despise you, and yet for weeks now all I've felt is this frantic need to lose everything, lose myself in the hot sorcery of your body.'

For a moment the pains swamped her, clutching at her heart with vicious talons. But she shivered, breaking free from it, refusing to accept it. For beneath the calculated cruelty of his words there had been a stark need, an admission that she had a power over him greater than any other woman. The knowledge was bitter to him but a glory to her. Tomorrow they would part as enemies, but when he remembered her, and he would, he would remember that she alone could make him groan out his need for her, strong body trembling with a hunger greater than the logic of his quick cold brain or his hard self-control. She had pierced the armour of his self-sufficiency; part of his hatred was because he was a proud man, and until she had come no other person had ever done that.

Her mouth curved as she let her head fall back on to the pillow. Her hands came up to his shoulders, and she pushed him away.

'No spell, no incantations,' she said huskily, her voice as soft as a moth's flight. 'See, I'm not holding you here. You're free to go.'

Against the starshine his shoulders loomed over her, dark before the paler oblong that revealed the position of the french windows. Arminel's eyes were accustomed to the faint radiance. She could see the taut line of his jaw, the dark hollows where his eyes burned, the movement in his throat as he swallowed. After a moment he swung away, pulling himself up to sit on the side of the bed. He sat motionless, shoulders hunched.

Arminel lay motionless while through her body the tide of desire flowed, suffusing every cell, every nerve, calling him back, promising him oblivion after raptures he could not even begin to imagine. She did not have to see him to know the forces that were tearing at him, pride warring with lust, anger and bitterness with a contempt he had to accept as directed towards himself.

If I loved him, she thought, I would be in agony for him. But I do not love him. It seemed important to cling to that belief.

From beneath her lowered lashes her eyes gleamed. And when he lost that battle with himself she knew before he swore and came with a lunge back on to the bed ready to use her in anger and a fierce despair.

Only to find that he could not. Somehow she knew that for him this was the greatest defeat; her body welcomed him and the harsh invasion was transformed into a taking and giving so erotically charged that when it reached its climax an identical storm of sensation broke over both of them.

How long did it take for strength to return? She never knew, content to lie relaxed in total release while slowly the beat of both hearts faded into regularity and the dawn crept closer.

Then they both slept, heart to heart, limbs entwined, covered by a sheet, as the birds sang in the new day, Arminel's last day at Te Nawe. Not that Arminel cared for that. She was capable of feeling only a sensual satiation that left her sleek and replete as though her body was made of velvet and silk, her mind long ceasing to struggle with logic and reason.

When she opened her eyes again it was against the dull grey light of dawn on a cloudy day. A rough grip on her shoulder shook her head from side to side; she felt a sharp stinging pain in her cheek as it was slapped. Wincing, her swollen lips pursed in protest, she opened heavy eyes and stared into Rhys's livid face.

'What——?' she muttered, covering her eyes with her hand as she struggled up on to her elbow. 'What is it? What's happened?'

'You ask *me* that?' His contempt flicked her on the

raw, making her wince again. 'From what Kyle said when I met him just now on his way to his own bedroom you've had a busy night. Fun?'

'Oh, God!' she breathed wearily, sinking back on to the pillow. This was worse than anything else Kyle had done to her; he had deliberately flung her to the wolves. And although it was only Rhys's pride that was hurt it was still painful for him. She could see the resentment and anger in his face now. Somehow she was going to have to make things better.

'Your brother is a bastard,' she said shakily, pushing her hair back from her face.

'And you're a bitch,' he remarked with unpleasant emphasis, watching the lines of her breast beneath the sheet. 'How long has it been going on, Arminel? Since you got here? You and Kyle must have had a lot of fun laughing at me!' He watched her flush and added cruelly, 'When can I expect an announcement of the engagement?'

'Don't be stupid,' she said, closing her eyes momentarily. 'You know as well as I do that Kyle doesn't think I'm good enough for you . . .'

'—and I'm inclined to agree with him,' he interpolated crudely.

'. . . so there's no likelihood of him doing anything stupid like marrying me,' she finished, adding with a smile that trembled, 'Just a bit of crumpet, I think that's the correct term, isn't it? And last night was the first, last and only time. I'm leaving today.'

Rhys stared down at her, then said coolly, 'Well, I think you're wise. You're quite right about Kyle, of course. He'll probably marry Patrice Gribble. If he offers to set you up in Auckland in return for visiting rights what will you say?'

She looked away. 'Do you really want to know?'

He nodded.

'I'll thank him prettily and say no. I want to go back home.'

'Fair enough.' Hands thrust into his pockets, he walked across the room, stopping at the doorway to say rather insolently, 'I'll write you a cheque for your air tickets. I don't want you to be out of pocket.'

'You needn't bother.' She could have flinched at the ring of arrogance in his voice, but although she was not a Beringer and did not move in their circles she had pride too. Her head lifted, her face was expressionless as she finished, 'I'll chalk it all up to experience. Good luck, Rhys.'

He hesitated, then said, 'For you, too,' and was gone. He even whistled as he passed Kyle's door.

Pride again. Well, he hadn't made such a bad job of salvaging his. In a year's time he would probably be happily reconciled to marriage with Davina and he'd barely be able to recall Arminel's face.

Choking back a sob, she turned her head into the pillow. In a year's time she probably wouldn't remember what Rhys looked like, but she knew that Kyle's features were indelibly engraved on her memory. And today she was leaving him for ever.

Last night had been a dream, an erotic fantasy from her over-stimulated imagination, wish-fulfilment. This cold grey dawn was the only reality. And she had to get up and face it with all the pride she could summon, because it was only pride which was going to get her through the day ahead.

So she got up and showered every inch of herself, washing hair still lank with sweat, consciously cleaning herself of every trace of the night. Then she dressed, pulling on jeans and a jersey the exact colour of her eyes darkened now to a bruised blue, dried her hair and tied it back from her face in a ponytail. The hairstyle emphasised the clear, strong lines of her face, making her look more severe yet, paradoxically, younger. Normally she wore nothing more than moisturiser in the day, but this morning she made up carefully, using a coloured base to hide her lack of colour, a rosy lipstick to disguise lips reddened from kisses which had been too deep.

It was after eight when she finally came out; she stood a moment in the doorway, looking hesitantly back at her bedroom, its vivid atmosphere like a refuge. Then she set off down towards the small room off the kitchen where breakfast and often lunch were eaten.

Mrs Beringer was there drinking tea as she read yesterday's paper. When Arminel entered she looked up, her expression coolly pleasant.

They exchanged greetings. Arminel sat down, fighting down nausea at the thought of food, and began on her usual breakfast, grapefruit and toast and coffee. Outside the day had cleared; the sky was a brilliant tender blue and all about were the sounds of Te Nawe, the faint purr of an engine, sheep crying, a dog barking hysterically, the comfortable clatter in the kitchen as Judy Caird moved about. A blackbird sang sweetly and loudly from the orchard and somewhere a tractor started up to the accompaniment of a shouted command.

Arminel fought back a surge of grief. After today this would all be in the country of the past. And she would never cease to regret being banished from it.

'Had you any plans for today?' Mrs Beringer asked politely.

Arminel shook her head. After a moment her throat loosened enough for her to say, 'No, none, except that I must confirm my ticket back home.'

'I see.' Not a sign of triumph in the cultured voice, yet it was there, as clear as if she had shouted it to the sky. 'When are you thinking of going back?'

'Oh, fairly soon.' Well, it had to be done. Buttering a piece of toast, she said quietly, 'I thought I might leave today, as a matter of fact. I've loved being here, but I'd like to see a little more of New Zealand before I go home.'

Mrs Beringer could afford to be generous now. 'Yes,

we have a lot to offer the tourist. Where are you thinking of going next? The South Island is lovely at this time of year, although of course it's seen at its best in winter when the snow is down.'

'I thought I'd go to Rotorua and have a look at the thermal area.'

'Yes, you must. It's unique and fascinating, once you get used to the smell of sulphur.'

Arminel smiled politely. She had no intention of going any further than Auckland and then she'd catch the next plane home to lick her wounds in solitude.

At the sudden opening of the door both women looked up. Kyle came in, his cold grey eyes passing from his mother's face to Arminel's with no discernible change of expression.

'I've just had a call from Auckland,' he said without preamble, addressing his mother. 'I have to go down to see Arthur Jolley—something's come up about the Gisborne place. I'll leave after lunch.'

'Oh, then you can give Arminel a lift,' Mrs Beringer said pleasantly. 'She was just saying that she thought she'd spent enough time here.'

'Indeed?'

Arminel's spine crawled at the mocking derision in the gaze that searched her face. 'Yes,' she said in a remote little voice, spreading marmalade on to her toast.

'Then feel free to accompany me.' He smiled. 'I like company.'

He was a ruthless, calculating devil and he was twisting the screw even harder, revenging himself for the sensual snare he had been caught in.

So although her heart and brain ached in unison she looked at him with polite detachment, the soft, passionate mouth tight above the delicate lift of her chin. 'Thank you. When do you plan to leave?'

'Straight after lunch. Can you be ready by then?'

'Yes.'

The shrewd grey eyes bored into the pretty mask of her face. He sensed her complete withdrawal and it angered him. But he hid it and turned to his mother.

'Where's Rhys?'

She looked up at him, her expression ingenuous. 'He decided to go to the village. You said last night that you wanted some parts for the pump. Davina has gone with him.' She paused before finishing, 'I think they intend calling in on Mary and Peter Goldstone. They'll probably stay for lunch.'

'I see.' His gaze swung to Arminel's face once more, met and locked with hers. A bitter, savage, triumph blazed deep in his eyes, then was extinguished as suddenly as it had come. 'Right, make it one o'clock,' he said as he turned towards the door.

So that was that. As she packed Arminel pushed all her anguish away from her, concentrating with fierce desperation on the job in hand. Only a few more hours and she would never see him again. Yesterday—even this morning—the thought had been as painful as a blow to the heart. Now she welcomed it. The future beckoned like a haven. Without the constant cruel torment of Kyle's presence she would pick up the pieces of her life and make something of it. And never again would she lay herself open to such humiliation and hurt. Nothing, not even the delirious physical enchantment of last night, was worth it. If he had despised her before he now felt a darker, stronger emotion for her, something that forced him to taunt her as cruelly as he knew how. And because he was Kyle, with a quick, incisive brain, he knew exactly how to shaft the arrows of his words.

Oh yes, she would be glad to see him walk away from her.

By mid-morning she was ready. It took her half an hour to write a note to Rhys. She would post it in Auckland; if she left it here she would be surprised if it reached its destination.

She smiled a cynical little smile, thinking that only a few weeks ago she would have been horrified at the thought of well-bred, well-to-do people like the Beringers stooping so low as to filch a letter. Well, she had grown up a lot since then. And until she saw the last of Kyle she would behave with a self-possession that was rooted in the depths of her disillusionment.

After that she went for a walk outside, visited Tessa and gave her an apple, patting the velvet muzzle as the little mare pressed her head against Arminel's. For a moment tears blinded her; she wiped them away with an angry hand and made her way down through the gardens, quickening towards summer now, drowsy in the soft air. Beneath them the land swooped gracefully down to the sea, no longer cold under a cold sky as it had been on her arrival. Now the water glimmered and beckoned and shone. In the summer, Rhys had told her, they had parties down on the beach, parties which lasted from lunchtime until after midnight. They swam and walked and sang, made love and cooked their food over coals from a bonfire, watching as the long breakers curled on to the beach and the fish in them were silhouetted momentarily against the hard pale summer sky.

Well, waiting for her were waters warmer than these would ever be, and a life she had found pleasant. It would be pleasant again, she promised herself. In time Kyle's ominous shadow over her happiness would diminish and this, too, would become a memory, painful, always tender to the touch, but no longer a part of every waking moment and every sleeping dream.

Resolution firmed her mouth. She turned and made her way back to the house to help Judy with the lunch.

It was a meal fraught with tension. Kyle was abstracted, eating quickly without appearing to taste his food. It was left to his mother to put some sort of social gloss over the situation. She managed it very well, all things considered. Arminel, for once the recipient of her hostess's conversation, responded in kind, giving polite meaningless answers to polite meaningless remarks.

When she said goodbye to Judy Caird a note of real emotion crept into her voice as she thanked her. Judy's look was shrewd, but she smiled and wished her a pleasant holiday in the rest of New Zealand.

An impatient toot from the horn of the car put an end to this. Mercifully Kyle's impatience to be gone kept farewells short. Mrs Beringer was gracious, Arminel smooth, and within a minute or so the big car slid quietly down the drive towards the cattle-stop. Arminel stared ahead, eyes blind, her whole mind filled with the image of the man whose strong hands manoeuvred the car so skilfully around the sharp, deeply gravelled corners.

Now, when she was leaving, she accepted the fact that what she felt for him was not a frenzied desire. Somehow she had fallen in love with him. Leaning her head back on to the seat, she wondered bleakly why it should be Kyle, hard and cruel and contemptuous, who had stolen her heart from her. Rhys was much easier to love—but no, her wayward heart had chosen his brother.

Partly because of his strength, that granite character which called to a like strength in her. She needed a strong man to love. Rhys had never evoked the response which flamed so swiftly for Kyle. Basically Rhys was lightweight, with all the virtues of that, the laughter and fun, the easy rapport which had first attracted her, but he was incapable of reaching the heights, or the depths. In time he would get over his chagrin at being manipulated and marry Davina; they were ideally suited, and her open adoration was what he needed.

Kyle was different. Dimly she realised that the antagonism which had flared between them at that first glance had been based on an intuitive need to protect themselves. Each had recognised in the other—what?

The capacity to hurt, to maim so deeply that the resultant wounds would scar their souls. All of it, the incandescent attraction, the dark bonds of desire and shame and hunger with violence only a kiss—or a blow—away, their unwilling, desperate joy in each other's presence, were parts of the dark chains that bonded them together.

Love? It seemed as far removed from the kindly emotion she had once dreamed of as the stars from the pits of hell, yet he would never forget her. If there had been mainly depths in her relationship with Kyle at least they both had one ecstatic height to remember.

Closing her eyes, she lost herself in memories until at last, to the background of music from the tape deck, she slept.

The Beringers owned a house in Remuera, an elegant, weatherboarded building, cared for superbly by another housekeeper. Kyle introduced them, then followed them up the stairs to the bedroom allotted to Arminel with her suitcase.

'I'll be back for dinner,' he told the housekeeper. The cold eyes searched Arminel's shuttered face. 'You look as though you could do with a rest.'

Blue lights gleamed in her hair as her head moved, was averted.

She thought he hesitated, but when her eyes slid to follow him he was on the way to the door, moving with the leashed relaxed strength which was as typical of him as his incisive brain and his splendid physical presence.

She smiled meaninglessly at the housekeeper, who was too well-mannered to reveal the rampant curiosity she must be feeling. 'I think I'll have a bath,' she said, surprised at the evenness of her voice.

'Very well. The bathroom is the next room down the hall. Would you like a cup of tea?'

'I'd love one.'

'I'll bring it up here, shall I?'

It tasted like nectar, stimulating enough to drive away her lassitude. Somehow she had to get through this evening and do it with dignity; when she got back home she could wallow in self-pity and bitterness and whatever emotions a broken heart brought in its train. How trite! Victorian misses suffered from broken hearts, not twentieth-century women. But the pain that gripped her seemed centred in her heart, a griping, dull ache. I can't bear it, she thought, staring blindly down into her empty teacup. A tight lump blocked her throat as her brain repeated endlessly, I can't bear it, I can't. . . .

But she had to because there was nothing else to do. Her life seemed an endless repetition of rejections great and small, from her parents' defections to this, the most painful and wounding. She had fought her way through the cold fear each one engendered, and she would do the same now, drawing on her reserves of strength. At the moment they seemed pitifully scant, but her head lifted proudly and she said aloud to the watchful room, 'I'll manage.'

Kyle didn't return for dinner.

'He asked me to give you his apologies,' the housekeeper told her. 'He's still at the office. Would you like your meal on a tray?'

'Yes, please.'

It was superbly cooked, so she forced herself to eat at least half of it. Later, she sat in an opulently furnished room and listened to music, choosing carefully so that the bitter pain that racked her wasn't reflected in the music. But even as the exquisitely joyous notes of a Chopin piece played by a master ravished her ears the slow tears formed and fell and she whispered, 'I wish I could die.'

Exhaustion must have overtaken her; when she awoke the room was silent, silent and cold and waiting, and she was stiff. Yawning, her hand pressed to a tightly throbbing temple, she walked towards the door.

Halfway up the stairs the click of a key in the front door jerked her head around. For a moment she stared down at him, ominous, his head tilted to watch her, his face impassive in the subdued light. Her hand tensed on the balustrade; it took a positive action of will to relax it and continue climbing, head held high, shoulders squared against the dark menace of his regard.

Once inside the room she relaxed, leaning against the dressing table as though she had run a marathon, one hand pressed against her wild heart. There were no footsteps to warn her. When the door opened she gasped and paled.

He stared at her, lashes hiding his emotions. 'You left the stereo on.'

'I'm sorry.' But the words were silent. She had to clear her throat and say them again, and all the time his gaze darkened and heated as it roved her face and the long gentle line of throat and breasts.

'I could make you sorrier,' he said unevenly, closing the door behind him.

She winced. 'Please go. I can't—I've had enough, Kyle.'

'I could make you weep for the day you were born.' He came towards her, ignoring her plea, until he stood a pace away. She could feel the dangerous instinct to hurt beating out from him, sledge-hammering into her form.

He smiled at her involuntary retreat and said deeply, 'Shall I do that, Arminel? I'd like to. I'd like to hurt you until you tremble at the thought of me and those tantalising red lips pale. I could, couldn't I?'

The pulse at the base of her throat fluttered with a speed that revealed her fear. His eyes fixed on to it until she thought that the skin burned and stung with the intensity of his gaze.

'Yes,' she whispered hopelessly. 'You know you could.'

Ferocious triumph sprang into his eyes. 'Why?'

Her lips were dry, her mouth parched. She shook her head Kyle smiled again, slowly, and pulled her towards him with hands that were cruel on her arms.

'Why?' he insisted remorselessly. 'Tell me why, you beautiful bitch, or I'll force it from you!'

Her lashes flickered. What black desire to humiliate was this? Her eyes slid sideways to the bed.

'Yes,' he said softly between his teeth. 'Like that, darling. Who knows what else I might force from you?'

Black hair swirled in a cloud about her shoulders as she flung her head up. Her face set in proud lines, her eyes flashing.

'Why?' he demanded, voice urgent with an unknown emotion.

'Because I love you,' she said clearly, her face challenging, almost exultant for one fierce second.

His chest lifted and fell. 'Yes,' he said. 'Why, Arminel?'

'Because I'm a fool. A poor fool.'

Again that slow, freezing smile. 'You are, indeed. If you hadn't been so greedy you might even have got yourself a rich husband. God knows, you're beautiful enough. But I dislike rapacious women. So do most other men. Remember that next time you get a rich one in your sights.'

She reacted to such mocking derision with a violent wrench at his wrists, but when her fingers touched his skin they curled around the strong bones, sliding over the places where his pulses beat, faster and more fast yet, betraying him.

His hand slid up her arm, over the slender bones of her shoulder to her throat. The long fingers tightened just enough to hurt. He bent his head. His hostility was open and stark, his mouth twisting as he saw the fearful submission in her expression.

'Kiss me, Arminel,' he ordered silkily.

There could be no further shame to inflict on her.

Slowly she lifted her head and moved her lips, lightly, sensuously, against his. Her body swayed and his mouth tightened.

'Goodbye, Kyle,' she whispered.

He smiled, his eyes gleaming like burnished steel. 'Not quite yet, darling.'

The kiss was almost tentative, totally unsatisfying. For a moment Arminel was rigid, her head pressed back, her hands clawing his, then she groaned into his mouth and relaxed, giving him the surrender he demanded.

Deep inside the slow sweet hunger burgeoned; she swayed, longing to be caught against his hard strength, but he held her away so that the hunger became an ache of frustration and she struck at him with her clenched fist.

'Gently, darling,' he taunted as he put up a hand to brush back a lock of hair from her cheek. His touch was deliberately sensuous, moving up to the vulnerable hollow at her temple before sliding into the thick black tresses and pulling her towards him. 'Is this what you want?'

His arousal sparked an answering torment in her nerve-ends. She turned her head into his hand, kissing the hard palm.

'Yes,' she said simply, the word a caress.

His mouth swooped, closing her eyes. 'I've never seen such eyes,' he murmured in a thick undertone. 'Like sapphires lit from within, star sapphires blue as the sky on a summer night.'

His voice quickened as his mouth travelled towards her ear. Between kisses he said, 'And skin like living satin, warm and glowing.'

As his teeth toyed with the lobe Arminel's pulses surged and began to race. Although every instinct she possessed warned her of her danger she could no more resist this seduction than she could stand up straight. Limp, held up only by the strength of his arms and the

support of his body, she melted against him, her hands
sliding around his neck to find their way into the
burnished crispness of hair and pull his head down to
meet hers in a kiss which began as a teasing ploy and
ended with both of them out of control.

'You drive me out of my mind,' he groaned as he
picked her up and laid her on the bed, then came down
beside her, a hand cupping the smooth curve of her
breast, his mouth at the hollow in her throat where a
frenzied pulse beat. Almost absently his thumb brushed
the hard promise of her nipple, before moving to the
small buttons of her shirt.

'You wear too many clothes,' he complained, but he
seemed to enjoy the process of taking them off. His
mouth swooped, explored the hollows of her shoulder
exposed by his probing fingers. As if unable to wait
until he had freed her completely from her clothes his
teeth sought the erect nub of her breast through the fine
material of her bra. Very gently he manipulated it for a
moment. Arminel's breath locked in her throat; her
hands clenched and a shudder shook her.

Kyle lifted his head and gave a curious, breathy laugh
before sliding his hand beneath her to free the clip of
her bra. Now he could see her, naked to the waistband
of her velvet skirt, the smooth globes of her breasts
inviting his mouth and his hands.

Against the soft skin he whispered, 'Would you stay
with me if I asked you, Arminel?'

Before she could answer his mouth moved and she
felt a long moan break through her lips as it fastened on
to her breast. Her body arched into a rigid bow. Sharp
stabs of sexual pleasure rendered her helpless. She
moaned again, holding his head against her.

'Well?' he asked.

'Can't you guess?' she asked bitterly, because of
course he knew, he knew exactly what he was doing to
her.

He laughed again, sliding his hand beneath the heavy

velvet of her skirt. Then he said nothing more, his hands and mouth saying it all for him until she lay naked in his arms, her head flung back, her body on fire for him as he tormented her with kisses which were agony, caresses which made her sob. His shirt had joined hers on the floor and he loomed over her, shoulders gleaming in the soft light, the scrolls of body hair tracing out the magnificent structure of chest and arms.

'Will you stay with me, Arminel?' he tempted, watching her through narrowed eyes which were lit by a flame.

'Yes.'

His mouth covered hers in a deep, thrusting kiss. Completely out of control, she pulled him down on to her until his body pressed hers into the bed.

'It will have to be here, in Auckland,' he whispered, sliding his hands down beneath her hips to prevent her withdrawal.

Arminel shook her head numbly, sickened by what he was offering her. Yet even before she answered she knew what it would be.

'Yes,' she said, the word acid on her tongue, her wild eyes agonised.

There was triumph in the half-closed eyes, triumph and something else. 'I'll find you a flat,' he said, 'and I'll be able to get down quite often to see you.' His face hardened. 'But I'm a possessive lover, so there'll be no other men.'

'Lover?' Defiance throbbed in her voice even as she ran her hands over the smooth width of his back, revelling in the way he trembled at her touch. 'Owner would be a better word!'

Kyle laughed and ran his hand from the bruised softness of her lips to her breasts and down, down, in a gesture as possessive as it was exciting.

'Do you like the thought of being owned by me?' he asked on a taunt. 'Owned body and soul and mind, mine do with as I wish, my slave bound to me by chains stronger than iron or steel?'

Her eyes, dark with fear, met the blazing heat of his. She could not sustain the look and turned her face into his shoulder. 'No, I hate it,' she responded huskily.

'But it excites you,' he jeered, and he knew, his experience told him just how much her body craved him. And he repeated the gesture he had made before, letting her feel the possession in his hand before he pushed himself away, saying quite calmly, 'But it doesn't excite me all that much, so perhaps you'd better catch that plane after all.'

She wasn't surprised. Every trace of colour fled her skin, but she was able to summon up some kind of strength and meet the savage derision of his expression without flinching, even though for a moment she thought she was going to faint. Beads of sweat broke through her skin and the beautiful, demonic mask of his face whirled and dipped. Her breath hurt her lungs; she lay like a marble statue while every vital process of her body seemed to halt.

She understood his need to humiliate her. The night before it had been he who lost control, she who had used the power of her sexuality to force him to surrender to it. To such a self-sufficient, dominant man this could only have made him a lesser man in his own estimation. His pride was hurt, his view of himself cheapened.

He would not know that she had not intended to shame him, her pleasure had been an almost innocent one in her own body and its allure. But she had shown him that she had power over him. Now he was doing the same to her, adding refinements of cruelty because he despised himself for his weakness.

But he wanted to kill her self-respect. She looked into his watchful eyes and said quietly, 'If you get off the bed I'll get into my nightdress.'

Only for a moment his expression revealed shock

before he rolled away and sat on the side of the bed. He didn't watch as she pulled on her nightdress and dressing gown. Arminel's whole body screamed with frustrated desire, but she forced herself to move with her usual deftness. There was nothing she could do to retrieve the situation.

As she went across to the dressing table he stood up and watched her, his expression completely without emotion, the strong bones of his face clenched as the aloof, dispassionate eyes slid over the delicate contours of her face.

Then he said, 'Congratulations, Arminel. You've got enough nerve to go a long way,' leaving her in no doubt that he understood the motivation behind her actions.

Slowly she stroked the brush through hair tangled by his fingers, her dark gaze steady as he stooped to pick up his shirt and walked out with it slung over his shoulder, the lean tapered body perfectly balanced. Even from across the room the physical magnetism brushed her nerves.

At the door he paused, half-turning to say impassively, 'I've booked you a seat on the Air New Zealand flight to Brisbane tomorrow morning. Be ready to leave by nine.'

The hard gaze raked her averted profile. 'Naturally Beringers is paying,' he finished.

She looked up. 'Not Rhys?' and could have bitten her tongue out at the mocking comprehension that sprang into his eyes.

'No, the firm. Did he offer to? Poor Arminel!'

Still smiling, he walked through the door, closing it noiselessly behind him.

When he had gone she removed her make-up and lay crouched in the bed. No tears came, no conscious thought. Nothing but a wrenching agony of heart and mind and body. It was not yet the time to weep for Kyle, weep for her lost innocence and the dark chains of a love gone wrong, weep for the years ahead when the sight of a tall man with shoulders wide enough to shut out the world and hair the colour of bronze would bring back the memory of this desolation and for a few moments she would be young and completely alone again.

The big jet was swooping down on to the coast of Australia when her voice tailed away into silence. She stared hopelessly into the almost empty glass he had ordered after the meal and insisted she drink. She was exhausted, her tones flat and dull, but she felt a little better for unburdening herself. Not that she had told him everything, of course, but she was sure that he was astute enough to read between the lines of her bald narrative.

Strange to have bared her soul to a complete stranger while all around was the quiet activity of stewardesses passing up and down the aisles, serving meals and taking orders for drinks. But then the whole thing had been strange, from her instant attraction to Rhys to the final traumatic scene with Kyle.

Her companion said drily, 'Well, my dear, I think you've earned the right to shed a few tears. What do you plan to do now?'

'Pick up the pieces.' A flash of spirit firmed her mouth. Painfully she continued, 'I'm not the only person to suffer from unrequited love, if that's what this is. I'll get over it. When I'm ninety I'll wonder why on earth I made such a fuss.'

Her answer pleased him, because he laughed softly and said, 'Ah, I knew you wouldn't let it sour you. Tell me, what are your immediate plans?'

'Kyle booked me into a hotel for a week.' She shrugged. 'I'll use the time to get a job.'

He insisted on taking her to the hotel and when he said goodbye wished her good luck. She waved after the departing taxi, then turned to follow the porter into the hotel. She would never know who he was, her unknown rescuer, but she would never forget him. He had been kind when she had almost forgotten that kindness existed.

That night she went out like a light, sleeping for twelve solid hours before waking with a headache and the swimmy sensations of one who needs food.

It took all her willpower to force down the meal she ordered, but starving herself was foolish.

After that she packed and went downstairs to tell the desk clerk that she was leaving.

'But, madam—Miss Lovett, the booking was for a week,' he protested. 'I hope you are not dissatisfied with us?'

'Of course not.' Impossible to tell him that she couldn't bear to accept Kyle's bounty. 'I've just changed my mind about staying, that's all.'

After finding herself a room in a boarding house well out of town she bought some newspapers and began to look for work.

As she had suspected, the following days proved that it was not easy. There were not many positions vacant, and those that were advertised had plenty of applicants. Although her qualifications and references were excellent employers jibbed at the knowledge that she had thrown up a perfectly good position to go to New Zealand. As one woman at an employment agency put it, it did seem to smack of some giddiness of purpose.

It didn't help that she was not sleeping. Not even make-up could hide the hollows in her cheeks or the indefinable air of weariness that clung to her. But she would not give in. If she couldn't get a job in an office then there were other things she could do, working in a shop, perhaps.

During the day she managed to ignore her grief, but at night she twisted in her narrow bed, her too-active brain recalling every time Kyle had touched her, every time his eyes had rested on her. Oh, she hated him, hated him and loved him, and she was eating her heart out for him.

After ten days or so she had some luck.

'It sounds ideal,' she said, trying to summon up some eagerness. 'In a lawyer's office?'

'Yes.' The woman at the agency gave her a strange look. 'Here's the address.'

It was a suite of offices on the thirtieth floor of one of Brisbane's modern buildings, very opulent, very hushed. But when the door opened into the interview room the man behind the desk was the man who had befriended her on the plane.

'Oh!' she gasped, sudden colour flooding her skin. 'Oh, it's you!'

He smiled, the shrewd, kind eyes noting her thinness, the shadows beneath her eyes and the tightness around her mouth. She had the impression that he could read everything that had happened, all the disappointments that had sapped her spirit. Her hands jerked in an involuntary movement, defensive, wary.

'Was this a set-up?' she asked.

He nodded, but as she made a blundering movement towards the door said quietly, 'Sit down, Arminel. I promise you that I have no evil intentions towards you.' And when she hesitated, he smiled, and she could see the tiredness behind it. 'Sit down, you silly child.'

The charm was there, the kind of gentleness that only the very strong possess. Numbly she sat down, her head lowered, her fingers nervously twisting the clasp on her bag while she waited for him to tell her why he had gone to all this trouble to meet her again.

'I should have realised that you wouldn't stay in the hotel a minute longer than necessary,' he began. 'I've had the devil's own job to trace you, and finally had to fall back on this. Do you realise that I've already interviewed two women for this non-existent position?'

Without raising her head she asked, 'Why? Why did you want to keep in touch with me? On the plane you said we'd never see each other again.'

'When I said that I intended it to be the truth,' he said calmly. 'Before I explain, have you heard from Kyle Beringer?'

The colour rushed from her cheeks, leaving her like a pale flower, broken in the wind. 'No,' she whispered, too tired to feel anything more than pain.

'I sent him a telegram purportedly from you, communicating your safe arrival,' he said with cool deliberation.

Her head jerked upright on the slender neck. Quick reviving anger lit the depths of her eyes. 'How dare you!' she choked, springing to her feet in a swift motion. 'Just who do you think you are! I—you had no right to do such a thing, poking your nose into my business! Just who are you?'

'That can wait,' he told her without emotion. 'Are you quite sure there's no hope? He's not likely to come haring across the Tasman after you when he's had a taste of life without you?'

It seemed easier to answer him. 'No,' she said, her mouth twisting. 'I told you, he threw me out.'

'The way you told it, he's in love with you.'

'No.' Wearily she shook her head. 'He hates me.'

'Sometimes the two go together.' But when she shook her head again he went on in a softer tone, 'Well, all right, but even if he hates you he must know there's the possibility of a child. Surely he wouldn't just abandon you.'

'He thought—he probably assumed that I took care of that,' she said with painful candour. 'He thought that—that I'd slept with Rhys. Anyway, there's no possibility now.' She lifted her head, met without flinching eyes which were suddenly very hard and piercing. 'Not that it would have made any difference. You don't know Kyle. Even if he does—did—love me, there's no way that he would let me set foot on the station again. I'm not suitable material for a Beringer wife. And there's nothing anyone could do to make him change his mind.' She looked down at the hands that were clenched in front of her body and lifted them, joined together in a parody of prayer. 'Do you think I didn't try?'

'I see.' And if the compression of his mouth was anything to go by he did indeed see, and didn't like what his imagination visualised. Well, she didn't like to recall such humiliation either, but it had one good result. Never again was she going to allow herself to get in such a position. She had humbled herself for the last time.

But she was tired, so tired that she felt as though nothing would ever be right again.

'I think that had he wanted to change his mind he'd have contacted you by now,' he said thoughtfully. 'I've had the hotel checked and there's been nothing. What do you think I was doing in New Zealand, Arminel?'

She collapsed into the chair again. 'I don't know,' she said, exhaustion robbing her voice of colour and vitality.

'I'd been to see a doctor in Auckland. After a battery of tests he confirmed a diagnosis I'd already heard here.' He spoke dispassionately, as though discussing a person neither known nor liked much. 'A diagnosis which says that I have a degenerative disease which is going to kill me in three or four years.'

Appalled, her horror dilating her eyes, she whispered, 'I'm so sorry, so sorry,' then fell silent, for in the face of his lack of emotion hers seemed excessive.

'I've had some months to live with it,' he said indifferently, though he was watching her keenly. 'And I've had a good life. There is only one thing that I regret. I have no children.' A deliberate pause, his eyes still holding hers, before he finished, 'So will you marry me, Arminel, and give me a son or a daughter?'

# CHAPTER SEVEN

'FELICE, Felice—where are you, darling?'

The child laughed, bounding out from behind a clump of banana palms, her head tipped back as she looked up into her mother's face.

Arminel's heart contracted. She looked so like Dan, this daughter of his, with the same strong features and wide mouth; the same strong will, too, her mother thought wryly as she picked her up and buried her face in the amber curls.

Although only just four, Felice was already making it quite clear that she was very much a personality in her own right.

'Have you found her?' That was Karen, hot in the Fijian sun, her round face brown and vital.

'She was hiding down in the banana grove.'

Karen grinned at Felice's mischievous glance over her mother's shoulder. 'Baggage,' she said affectionately, and tweaked a curl. 'Time for your sleep, sweetie. Are you going to let Auntie Karen sing you a lullaby?'

'Ten green bottles?' Felice asked cunningly.

Karen laughed even as she pulled a face. 'Oh, very well, even though it's far too long. Come on, brat.'

Ten minutes later she came out and flopped on to a lounger beneath the shade of a corallita vine. 'Sound asleep,' she told Arminel. 'Gosh, she's a real ball of fire. All that energy!'

'Like her father,' Arminel said softly.

Karen looked across at her, her eyes considering. Three years as Dan Evans' wife and two as his widow hadn't made much difference to Arminel apart from a surface gloss which was the product of his great wealth. The woman who lay back beside the swimming pool was much the same as the girl who had grown up with Karen in the home. Stronger, less ebullient, her natural reserve had intensified so that even those who whispered that she had married for money and position didn't dare to say so to her face. Grafted on to the disturbing beauty was dignity and a poise earned by self-confidence.

'You still miss him, don't you,' said Karen.

Arminel nodded. 'Oh yes, every day.'

'Is that why you show no interest in any other man? And don't answer that if you don't want to.'

Even after all these years it hurt. Strange, for she had been so sure that the violence of the emotion must lead to its early death. But Kyle Beringer's image still prevented any other man from taking his place in her heart.

'No,' Arminel said quietly. 'Most of the men who want me come with dollar signs in their eyes.'

'Oh, rubbish! You know, you've got a fixation about the money. If you can believe that I like you for yourself, why be such a cynic about men?' Karen demanded with the robust common sense which made Arminel so fond of her.

'My dear, you were my friend before I married a millionaire. You are about the only person I trust completely to have my interests at heart.'

'Truly?' Karen was horrified. 'But what about all the advisers who watch over you so carefully? Dan must have trusted them to care for you?'

'So much so that he made sure they all watch each other and I watch them,' Arminel informed her drily. 'Dan had no illusions, believe me. He did his best for me and for Felice, but he would be the first to admit that the only certainty in this life is death.'

Karen's dark curls gleamed when she nodded. Her three years as Arminel's social secretary and companion meant that she had some idea of her employer's financial status but none of the ramifications of the trust which controlled her income.

Aloud she asked, 'Why did you marry him, Arminel? I know it wasn't the money.'

Arminel sighed. 'I—well, I suppose it was pity,' she said quietly. 'He told me about his condition and that he wanted a child.' She smiled with irony. 'I didn't, of course, realise how determined he was, or how ruthless. He quite deliberately played on my compassion. And I was at a—at a low ebb just then. He was kind, so kind when I needed kindness that I found myself married before I knew where I was.'

'He was an odd mixture, wasn't he?' Karen remarked, remembering.

Odd? No, Dan Evans just knew what he wanted and let nothing stand in his way, not even his approaching death. Arminel realised now, as she had not then, how skilfully he had played on her compassion and her weary desolation to pressure her into marrying him. It was not until some months later that she realised that he loved her with the desperate anguished love of a young man. Not that it would have made any difference to her decision. She would have still married him, forced into it by her intolerable need for someone to love her. He had been a gentle, considerate husband and lover, using his immense expertise to overcome her initial shyness and tension, but after Felice's birth his illness had prevented him from being a lover to her.

Secretly she had been unable to prevent herself from feeling a slight relief; if Dan knew of it he gave no indication but continued calm and good-humoured until his heart stopped one day as he was being prepared for bed.

Arminel had mourned him sincerely and long, emerging from her grief to discover that she was a very rich widow and therefore immensely eligible.

Not that any of the suitors who flocked to her side received any encouragement. Somewhat to the surprise of those cynics who assumed that they knew why she had married Dan, she neither took a lover nor showed any interest in remarriage.

'Was he disappointed that Felice was a girl?' Karen asked.

'Not in the least,' Arminel grinned. 'He took one look at her and laughed and said, "My God, I hope she's as tough as she looks!" and loved her.'

'Why don't you want to marry again? And don't give me any rubbish about them being after your money, because you know that Guy Cooper for one is besotted with you, and has more than enough money of his own to care about yours. And he's not the only one. You're absolutely beautiful, you always have been; even at the home we used to have trouble with boys. If I looked like you I'd have a ball, but you almost seem frightened of your face.'

Astute of Karen. 'Looks aren't everything,' Arminel returned vaguely. 'And I don't want another man. I'm perfectly happy the way I am.'

Lies, of course. Five years ago she had fallen in love with Kyle Beringer and she was still in love with him, so much so that his face haunted her dreams and no day went past that she didn't long for him with an emotion that was physical in its intensity.

Five years! Apart from the patient Griselda of legend she must hold some sort of record, she thought grimly. Not the kind to get her into the Guinness Book of Records, but if they had a book of fools she'd be a certainty for inclusion!

He was probably married by now, to Patrice Gribble or someone like her, someone sleek and sophisticated whose father had money and whose boarding school had concentrated on turning out young ladies, someone who had only had a job because life was dull without one. No doubt there were children, she thought, hugging the weapon of her thoughts to her breast, children who looked as much like Kyle as Felice looked like her father.

Stupid, sudden tears formed little rainbows across her lashes. From somewhere one of the Fijians began to sing, just a few phrases in a deep voice before he went back to sleep. Here in this enchanted hideaway in the islands everyone, even the people who came here as visitors, believed devoutly in the siesta.

Karen yawned. 'Are you still going along to the Goudges'?'

'*We* are still going,' Arminel told her.

'Oh, lord, must I? They're too—too society for me.' By which she meant that although perfectly pleasant Helen Goudge never let Karen forget that she was only in their charmed circle by virtue of her job.

Arminel smiled heartlessly. 'We did accept for both of us.' Then she relented. 'Well, I suppose I can produce a headache for you as it's not dinner. Although I believe they've got a visitor. Male. And according to Asena the sort of man to make your legs shake.'

'Asena is incorrigible,' Karen said sleepily. 'I mean, she's got Samuela, who must be the handsomest man I've seen in some years, but that doesn't stop her from eyeing every other man in the place, resident or visitor, up and down.'

'When you're married to someone who looks like Samuela you've got to keep them on their toes,' Arminel told her.

The sun rolled quietly across the sky in lazy tropical splendour while even the birds slept, in the breadfruit trees and in coconut palms and the canopy of the mango trees. No breeze cooled the long volcanic island which rose steeply to a ridge behind the wide flat area of the coconut plantation.

Because he had seen its potential Dan had bought it years ago and set about developing it with skill and a loving care which made it something unique. Set within Fiji's barrier reef, it was far enough from the main island to be isolated, close enough to make sure that life had no awkwardnesses.

The people lived or stayed on it had been carefully chosen. Mostly very rich, they inhabited houses as

varied as each owner, all set in acres of coconut palms
and exquisite gardens. Each year Arminel came here to
relax. It was a kind of pilgrimage, for Dan had loved it
most of all of his houses.

Now she slept while the sky blazed down and the sea
murmured gently and the perfume of frangipani and
ylang-ylang floated on the drowsy air.

Later that evening she and a resigned Karen walked
along the crushed coral path which led to the Goudges'
fantastic home.

'Mind you, I'm only coming because of Asena's
man,' Karen said cheerfully. 'How do I look?'

'Stunning!' And indeed she did, her bronzed prettiness
emphasised by the fine cotton caftan she wore in shades
of rose and peach and gold.

'While you, of course, look superb,' Karen told her
blithely. 'White makes you look like a queen.'

Arminel smiled. Her dress bore all of the hallmarks
of expensive simplicity, a fine linen with a dirndl skirt
and a little side-buttoning top that hid her waist, still as
narrow as it had been before Felice came. Against the
pristine clarity of the material her skin gleamed pale
gold; she wore no jewellery apart from her gold
wedding ring and small gold ear studs, but she had used
gold eye-shadow to emphasise her eyes and she wore
her favourite perfume, 'Ivoire', its haunting scent
evoking the mystery of the South Seas.

'I wonder what Helen will wear?' she wondered idly,
not really caring.

Karen snorted. 'If the man's as hunky as Asena says
it will be something really startling.'

Asena hadn't exaggerated. Helen had pulled out all the
stops, draping her long lovely legs in Capri pants in gold
and black which she topped with a short tunic in scarlet
silk. Around her neck she wore a barbaric necklace of
gold and black and dangling from her ears were great gold
leaves. Startling enough, but it was not she who made
Arminel draw a deep, harsh breath and falter in her stride.

Only for a moment, although her heart felt as though it was being squeezed in an iron fist. For it was Kyle who rose as Helen brought them out on to the wide terrace, and took her hand and said in a deep imperturbable voice,

'You don't need to introduce us, Helen, Arminel and I are old friends.'

'Really?' Helen's eyes were not the only ones avid with curiosity. 'Trust you, Arminel! How long have you known each other?'

He lifted Arminel's hand and kissed the back of it, the pale eyes coldly satisfied as they surveyed her pinched face.

'We met five years ago,' Arminel said huskily while her fingers crooked into claws.

'You must have been a baby.'

Arminel smiled, saying deliberately, 'It was just before I met Dan. I was nineteen.'

And drew blood. His eyes narrowed, but not until she saw the blaze of some dark emotion before he released her hand and was being charming to Karen, quite deliberately dazzling her as he did Helen, using that virile masculine charisma to reduce them to willing slavery.

By the time Tim Goudge had got them drinks and conversation became general once more Arminel had regained her poise, or the outward appearance of it. Amazing what you could do even when you felt as though you had been hit between the eyes with a hammer. Only the tiniest catspaw across the surface of her drink revealed that her hand was trembling, and under the cloak of self-command she was in such pain that it took all her strength not to cry out. Beneath the sun's kiss her skin was pale and clammy. For a moment there she had thought that she was going to faint—when Kyle had lifted her hand to his mouth her whole body had shouted its recognition of his touch and he had known it. His eyes had glittered with a savage triumph.

But not now. Slowly she concentrated, forcing her body to obey her will, the blood to return, bringing with it colour and a vitality which only she knew to be forced.

Karen had recognised the name, of course, and after one quick, puzzled glance she had shifted attention her way, sparkling, flirting a little too obviously with him, much to Helen's indignation. But it had given Arminel a much-needed breathing space so that when the conversation came her way again she was ready for it, the social mask firmly in place.

'I saw Felice snorkelling with you this morning,' Helen said. 'She's incredibly good in the water, isn't she? It's not often you see children of four who can swim like little eels.' She turned to Kyle. 'Felice is Arminel's daughter. Felice Evans, Dan Evans' child. You'll have heard of our poor sweet Dan, of course.'

'Of course.' The cool grey eyes swept Arminel's face and body. 'One of the biggest industrialists in the southern hemisphere. I'm sure everyone must have heard of him.' The insult was subtle, finding its way beneath Arminel's armour.

'He was a darling,' Helen said brightly. 'And Arminel is a truly devoted widow. Their marriage was such a romance. They met and were married within three weeks.' She laughed, a tinkling, empty little sound, before she continued, 'Of course, all his friends thought he'd gone quite dippy.'

'Arminel made him happy,' Karen interposed, a little fiercely.

Helen stared at her. 'Well, that's what I'm saying, my dear. I've never seen a man so thrilled as Dan was when Felice was born. A pity you couldn't have had a son, Arminel, but I must say no one would ever have known that he was disappointed, if he was.'

Helen was not particularly clever, but she had given her Tim three sons and perhaps more importantly had kept her figure. In spite of her shallowness she was a likeable soul, so Arminel smiled and said,

'I don't think he was disappointed.'

She lifted her glass and swallowed some of her drink, wishing that for once she had allowed Tim to get her something stronger than the lime juice and Perrier which was all that she usually drank. At this moment she could do with the artificial stimulus of alcohol. Her brain felt thick and woolly and she was only too conscious of the whip of Kyle's glance on her.

The Goudges had built their holiday home of great logs with an enormous thatched roof and a patio made of rounds of wood sunk into the ground, separated by clumps of low creeping plants. Helen loved gardens and hers was magnificent with hibiscus especially imported from Hawaii and great swathes of bougainvillaea against a dark, lush background of tropical foliage. Pots of amaryllis and mock azalea joined the brilliant stars of ixora and the musk-scented trumpets of datura to form an extravagant, fabulous atmosphere.

Now, with the sun down the patio was illuminated by flares. One side was shaded by a banyan tree, its leaves an enormous crown of rumpled green silk, but it was the frangipani that perfumed the air so sweetly, combining with gardenias and ginger and ylang-ylang in a sensuous exotic ambience.

Another couple arrived and then two adolescent sisters from a mile or so away who said they had been walking off restlessness. On any other occasion Arminel would have found amusing the way they took one look at Kyle and reacted like a starving woman before food, but tonight their open admiration tore at her nerves, making her jumpy and fretful until she felt that if she didn't get out of the place soon she would make a complete fool of herself.

By then it was turning into a full-scale party. Tim put music on and the beat reverberating through the tall palms attracted the local celebrity, a television personality from Australia who brought with him a film star friend from Hollywood, and a famous

Shakespearean actor. The teenage girls were ecstatic, but it was clear that they preferred Kyle's brand of unforced virility to the somewhat artificial glamour of the other three.

Arminel was disgusted to find herself watching them as they vied for his attention. An intolerable anguish gripped her in its coils. Why had she never been able to fight free of this dark enchantment he had laid on her? She had taken one look at him and fallen, headlong and for ever, under his spell. At first it had been physical attraction, but she had learned to love him, and in spite of all that had happened between them and the long years of parting that love was as strong as ever.

And Kyle? Once Dan had said that he had acted like a man in love. Perhaps he had been, but too much had happened to allow him to trust to his emotions. He had thought her a woman who wanted to marry money, trading the beauty of her face and form for the security. Her marriage to Dan could only have reinforced that belief. An ironic smile touched the warm curve of her mouth. Dan had made it possible for her to disabuse his mind of that illusion, but Kyle would have to ask her to marry him before he learned of the proviso in Dan's will that cut off every source of income from her if she married again.

And Kyle would never trust her, or his own emotions, enough to ask her to marry him. Even if he still loved her. If he had ever loved her.

Her eyes took in his physical perfection with wistful awe. How did he do it? Standing there, a half-empty glass in his hand, head slightly bent as he talked to the film star, he dominated this assembly of rich, beautiful people. Hungrily she took in the way his bronze hair gleamed as it covered the beautiful shape of his head, the stark strength of bone structure, austere and perfect beneath fine tanned skin, the thick dark lashes shielding eyes so clear that you would swear they could hide nothing, the arrogant strength of jaw, the mouth which could bruise and caress almost at the same time, severe and yet totally sensuous.

I love you, she thought, and as if her longing had been shouted aloud he looked up and tension sparked across the warm air like forked lightning, brilliant, deadly. For a long moment their eyes clashed until, trembling, she turned away. After a word with Karen she would slip away quietly, so quietly that no one would notice her absence.

Unfortunately she was waylaid, first by the television personality, whom she liked, even if he did overdo the amorous innuendo, and then by the actor who showed every sign of being smitten by her. He was also slightly drunk and more than a little conceited, but she was polite, parrying his compliments with a kind of dry amusement that astonished him.

'It's our strange Antipodean humour,' came Kyle's voice from behind her. He slid an arm around Arminel's waist and pulled her close, ignoring the sudden rigidity of her body as he continued easily, 'You have to be born in the Pacific if you want to understand it.'

'I see,' the actor said, and he thought he did see, his eyes shrewd as they went from Arminel to Kyle. 'Like our English jokes. Well, no doubt we'll see more of each other, Mrs Evans. I love your island.'

'It's not my island,' she said quietly, but he gave her the crooked smile he had used to such effect in several extremely good films and made his departure, setting his sights on one of the young women who had been trying to attract Kyle.

When he was a few steps away Arminel moved away. Kyle's arm dropped and he too smiled, not a pleasant smile.

'What it is to be a beautiful, rich widow,' he jeered softly.

She lifted her head back. 'What it is to be a beautiful, rich bachelor,' she parried harshly, her expression inexpressibly remote. 'Or are you married now?'

Again she had succeeded in startling him. His mouth tightened, then relaxed. 'No. You've developed a nasty tongue since last we saw each other, darling. Wasn't your marriage as idyllic as Helen thinks? Did you sharpen your tongue on your poor fool of a husband?'

'My marriage is no concern of yours,' she returned icily.

'It didn't take you long to crawl into someone else's bed,' he said with crude directness, finding pleasure in her quick shocked reaction. 'How old is your daughter?'

'She turned four two months ago,' she replied, refusing to allow herself to feel the insult.

'So she was conceived a month after you begged to be my mistress, vowing eternal love for me,' he said contemptuously. 'Eternity didn't last very long, did it? Tell me, were you as responsive, as wildly uninhibited in his bed as you were in mine?'

Arminel drew a deep breath, her face shuttered as she matched his contempt with her own. 'I don't have to justify my behaviour to you or anyone,' she said on a ragged note. 'You may have forgotten that you humiliated me before you threw me out of your life. You tried to destroy my self-respect. You have no right to judge me—you never did. Not,' she added with icy composure, 'when your own actions were hardly above reproach.'

The wide shoulders stiffened. He looked above her head at some distant vision, his expression rigidly remote.

'Do you think I don't know that? I went crazy, I think.' And in a totally different voice, lazy, almost casual and very much at odds with his watchful glance, 'Rhys is married.'

'To Davina, of course.'

'Of course. They were always perfectly suited. They married about eighteen months after your—after I became your lover.' The deep tones had a silky, sneering quality that struck at her poise. 'Tell me, how did you manage to convince your husband that you were still a virgin? From all that I've heard he was too experienced not to know the difference.'

'I didn't,' she said shortly. 'He knew.'

'Oh? Did you confess all? Clever girl!' But beneath the tan he was slightly pale as though her words had shaken him.

'Of course I told him.' Her swift glance slid away from his face to rest on her hands, trembling slightly.

'And he still wanted you?'

She wanted to hurt him, shake him from his height of arrogant disdain. Very softly she asked, 'Why should he not, Kyle? Dan was a mature, sophisticated man with a vast experience of life. He had no rigid, preconceived ideas of how people should behave. And he could certainly see the unfairness in the double standard.'

'Wise Daniel,' he said disagreeably. 'Did his tolerance extend to welcoming my child if you'd been pregnant? Or did he make sure that there was no possibility of that before he married you?'

She was shaken by his question. A warning flicked in her brain. 'By the time he asked me, I knew . . . that is . . .' She straightened up, lifting eyes which were deep-shadowed. 'There was no reason for him to make sure,' she said coldly. 'Felice is his.'

'I know that. I must admit I did wonder, but the date of her birth convinced me.'

Foolishly she snapped, 'Not that you cared!'

'Not particularly.' The indifference in his voice made her flinch before he added, 'Abortions are easy enough to get in Australia.'

'You really are a swine—a barbarian!'

He laughed and lowered his head so that his breath fanned warmly across her forehead. 'So you told me often enough at Te Nawe. Why the disappointment? Did you think five years would have changed me?' As she shook her head he said, 'Not at all, Arminel. I'm still the same swine you wanted then. Have you changed?'

For a moment she stood staring up at him, her eyes held by the mesmeric sheen of his. The lights from the flares flickered and shone, picking out the hard bone-structure of his face, the ruthless jaw and strong nose, the mouth which could kiss the heart from a woman or calmly say words to kill her. The physical attraction was as potent as ever.

Tension tightened its cords between them. Arminel took a deep sobbing breath and dragged her eyes from his, looking over his shoulder to see Helen approaching.

'Tell me about Rhys,' she said, turning half away.

He understood, of course. That watchful, waiting attitude left him; he smiled and said, 'Oh, he's fine. They live on the stud farm out of Cambridge with their two children—both girls, cute little creatures. Rhys wallows in quite undeserved devotion.'

Like her he turned so that he could see where Helen had been detained. 'Your quick marriage to the plutocrat cheered him no end,' he finished unpleasantly as his smoky eyes searched her face. 'He thoroughly enjoyed taunting me about your swift change of heart. It helped his ego considerably.'

'Good,' she said viciously, knowing that she was betraying herself and yet unable to do anything to stop it.

'Careful, darling,' he mocked. 'You'll have me thinking that you still hate me for throwing you out.'

'Hate you?' She moved away from the danger his lean body represented until the balustrade brought her up short. 'No, I don't hate you. I feel nothing for you. Five years is too long a time to hold a grudge.'

She set her glass down on the balustrade.

'Well, my feelings towards you haven't changed at all,' he said softly, watching her. When she said nothing he moved closer, blocking her from the rest of the terrace.

One hand touched her throat, lingered there, and as she drew in a frightened breath Kyle laughed low in his throat and picked up one of her trembling hands, raising it to his mouth to kiss the inside of her wrist.

Arminel's heart pounded in her breast. Without taking his eyes from her he said, 'We were good together, you and I. It seems a pity to throw that away, don't you think?'

'I'm not looking for a lover,' she said, each word delivered with brittle, pointed emphasis. 'When I am I'll remember you, don't worry.'

She stepped past him and he let her go, the golden flare of the torches illuminating his cynical smile.

'Enjoy your holiday,' she threw over her shoulder as she walked towards her hostess, holding her back so stiffly that her neck ached.

It was easy enough to slip away through the long grey trunks of the palms. Easy enough to press her fist to her mouth as the tears trickled down her face in the big shadowy bedroom after she had checked Felice; impossible to repress longings she had hoped were buried for ever. She spent all night fighting memories that left her spent and exhausted, lying in the wide empty double bed staring with dry, hot eyes at the ceiling while she wondered miserably if the pain ever ended.

But self-pity was a despicable emotion, and the dawn brought an end to it. Felice and she ate breakfast together, then set off down to the beach, the child slim and strong in her little yellow bathing suit beneath the enormous straw hat she had to be coaxed to wear. Goggles and snorkels and flippers hung from her arms; she sang a cheerful tune as she skipped ahead and when they came out on to the glittering coarse white coral sand she gave a wordless little cry of pleasure.

So early in the morning they had the place to themselves except for a *takia*, a small native sailing canoe out in the bay. One of the Fijians on his way home after a night spent fishing, probably.

Coconut palms and vai-vai trees lined the beach, the elegant palms leaning towards the water. Although it was so early the sun was warm and the water like silk.

'Come on, Mummy!' Felice called urgently from the edge of the sand.

'Coming!' Arminel hadn't even realised that her eyes had been scanning the beach in quick, suspicious movements. Of course he wouldn't be up. Karen hadn't arrived home until about three, but even after that the faint beat of the music had throbbed through the palms. No one at the Goudges' would be up so early.

So she relaxed and helped Felice with her flippers, then took her hand as they walked like ducks into a sea so glassy that it was impossible to see where the sand ended and the water began.

The reef was too far out for them to swim to, but there were coral outcrops in the bay and around them were the reef fish, living jewels with their expressive names, the demoiselles as blue as sapphires, moorish idols and brown tangs, yellow surgeons and black angels. The coral was an exquisite living sculpture, fit playground for the darting brilliant fish.

After twenty minutes Arminel touched her daughter's sleek brown shoulder and jerked her head towards the beach. Beneath the goggles Felice's frown was expressive, but she accompanied her mother in without cavilling. Strong-willed she might be, and prone to the occasional tantrum, but she knew that her daily sojourn in this fairyland depended on her obedience.

Back on the sand they sat in the little curling waves and took off their flippers and goggles, talking quietly—until Felice squinted up and said, 'There's a man coming, Mummy.'

## CHAPTER EIGHT

EVEN before she turned Arminel knew who it was; every nerve in her body was tensed as he approached, and she wished frantically that she hadn't chosen to wear a maillot that fitted like a second skin and plunged to an alarming degree both fore and aft. Its turquoise colour made her skin and hair glow, but she should have stuck to something that didn't reveal so much.

'Hello,' said Kyle, his expression well under control.

Felice looked at him doubtfully, but when her mother returned the greeting her little face relaxed into its usual cheerful interest.

'You must be Felice,' said Kyle, dropping on to his haunches in front of her.

The sun gleamed on his torso, picking out the flexing muscles beneath the skin. He was wearing nothing more than an old, faded pair of denim shorts. Hastily Arminel averted her eyes as her mouth dried.

'Yes.' Felice stood up and took a couple of steps towards him, her hands behind her back. 'What's your name?'

'Kyle.'

The clustering curls glittered as she nodded, gazing at him with her mother's eyes. 'Do you know my mummy?'

His gaze shifted, hardened as it impaled Arminel's. 'Yes, very well,' he answered.

Felice nodded again, watching him curiously with the open innocent assessment of childhood. 'Where are you staying?'

'With Helen and Tim Goudge.'

Arminel protested, 'Darling, that's enough! You mustn't ask so many questions.'

139

'How else is she to find out?' Kyle got to his feet, towering over them both, then extended a hand. 'Come on, get up. You can't stay sitting in the water like a mermaid for ever.'

She got up without any help, suffered his slow, taunting appraisal in impotent anger and said, 'We were just going up.'

'Are you going to offer me something to drink? There's not a soul stirring at the Goudges' and I'm dying of thirst.'

Arminel looked at him in silent hostility, but Felice answered for her. 'Yes, come up and have some coffee. Mummy likes coffee, but I don't.'

'No?' Kyle lifted a quizzical brow. 'What do you like?'

'Water. And milk.'

Picking up the snorkelling paraphernalia in one hand, he held out the other, and Arminel watched in astonishment as her daughter took it. But why should she be so surprised? This was just an extension of his formidable charisma. Apparently it affected any female, not only those who were nubile.

'You're very quiet this morning,' he said. 'Didn't you sleep well last night?'

She had seen the quick glance at the shadows under her eyes. 'Too well,' she lied. 'I always feel headachy if I've slept too heavily.'

It would have been better to admit the truth. His smile was openly sceptical, but he said nothing more until they reached the house.

Then he looked around, flagrantly evaluating the place, his gaze finally coming back to his reluctant hostess. 'Very—opulent,' he drawled unpleasantly. 'It suits you. Did your husband build it for you?'

'No.' She was determined not to be provoked. 'Just dump those there, will you, and come on in.'

The floor was ceramic tiles, cool and pale and easy for Asena to sweep clean of sand. Arminel led the way to where they ate beneath a rondavel beside the pool, and there was Karen, yawning, clearly not particularly surprised at Kyle's appearance.

'Hi,' she smiled. 'How are you? Super party, wasn't it?'

'Wasn't it?' His answering smile was a masterpiece, friendly, worldly and making it quite clear that he enjoyed the sight of Karen's curvy form attired in a brief scarlet bikini with a gold chain emphasising her waist.

'Kyle's come for coffee,' said Arminel in her coollest hostess's voice. 'And you could probably tempt him with some pawpaw or mango, Karen.'

'There's toast, too,' Felice offered cheerfully. 'Do you want some bacon?'

He grimaced. 'No, thanks, I'll stick to toast and coffee.'

Karen chuckled. 'Oh, come now, you can't have a hangover! You weren't drinking much. Boy, I'll bet there are several nursing sore heads this morning!' She named the actor, continuing cheerfully, 'He wanted to know all about you, Arminel.'

'Did he, indeed?' Arminel felt as though this was the last straw. As she poured coffee she said on a grim note, 'I hope you fended him off.'

'Sure. Told him that you valued privacy only slightly less than you valued your life and that anyone who stayed here had better learn it quickly. He's a bit full of himself, isn't he? Nice-looking, though, and that *fabulous* voice, like dark velvet!'

Kyle made some teasing remark and their laughter blended. Felice grinned happily as she picked up a slice of pawpaw and attacked the glistening apricot flesh. From the pool the sun's reflection shimmered up at them and the fresh warm morning air caressed their bodies, potent as a sorcerer's love philtre. Arminel looked down at her coffee and felt like screaming at the top of her voice. In fact she visualised the scene. Karen would be horrified, Felice frightened. And Kyle? Oh, he would smile in that half-mocking, disagreeable way and understand exactly why she was impelled to lose control so disastrously.

How dared he? How dared he come here and look at her with his cruel beautiful eyes and tell her without words that he felt nothing for her but scorn and disdain and a lust which was an insult.

'Mummy,' Felice said patiently, 'Mummy, can I go?'

'What, darling?'

Felice sighed, looking at Kyle with a resigned tolerance, 'Sometimes she goes off into dreams,' she explained. 'Mummy, Kyle's going up to the look-out point tomorrow. Can I go too?'

Arminel found no help from Kyle. From above his coffee cup his eyes mocked her.

'Oh, darling, no. Kyle won't——'

'He *said* I could.'

Damn you, her glance said. Aloud she protested, 'But it's such a long way. You'll get awfully tired.'

'I can ride. He's going up on one of the horses.' Felice's little face was pleading. 'Why don't you come too, Mummy, and Karen? We can take our lunches with us and the glasses for seeing through. Oh, *please*, Mummy!'

'Why not?' said Kyle, setting his cup down. 'It sounds to me like a pleasant way to spend a day. And as far as Helen's concerned, the more the merrier.'

Karen said nothing, but it was quite clear that she wanted very much to go. Arminel smoothed the frown from between her brows. Kyle had her in a spot and he knew it, and the best way to deny him full enjoyment of this form of harassment was to ignore it.

'Why not?' she said lightly. 'Have you organised the horses, Kyle, or would you like me to cope with yours as well as ours?'

'I'll do that,' he told her quite pleasantly, but when he left Karen giggled and said, 'Well, I know now never to offer to do anything for him. That is one very macho man.'

'Oh, you're so right.'

'Clearly you and he didn't get on five years ago and you're not going to try now.' Karen leaned her chin on the heel of her hand and viewed Arminel contemplatively. 'Which is a pity, because I rather think he has a yen for you.'

'Rubbish,' Arminel told her, steadying her voice. 'We don't like each other much.'

'But you're both too well-mannered to let it show?' Karen grinned. 'He seemed rather taken with Felice, and she with him.'

Which had surprised Arminel too; normally Felice treated strangers with a wary reserve until she knew them well enough to admit them into her friendship, or not, as the case was. But she had certainly opened up for Kyle.

'He is a menace to womanhood,' Karen said dreamily. 'But oh, what a *gorgeous* menace! If he didn't make it so perfectly clear that there is absolutely nothing doing I'd try for him myself. He makes my toes curl. You should have seen them all trying last night, the McLauchlan sisters especially, all fluttering lashes and lascivious dancing, and he was *so* charming and none of them got anywhere! Why do some men make all others look like shadows?'

'Because they're stuffed with male arrogance,' Arminel snapped. 'And stupid women think it's a sign of—oh, forget it!' She produced an unconvincing smile. 'He's got looks and strength and he's as sexy as hell, but there's no gentleness there, no kindness. If you're looking for a lover choose one with some consideration, even if he's not as seething with machismo.'

'Well, I haven't got a chance with him, anyway,' Karen said frankly. 'Oh, he flirts very nicely, but it's you he's got his eye on. Now, what's to be done today? I know there's a stack of letters waiting for answers.'

Plenty, fortunately, and after lunch they slept. Then Felice insisted on a shell-collecting trip, so they wandered along the beach in the opposite direction from the Goudge house before playing a fairly hectic game of chase through the palms.

After a prolonged dinner Arminel read some of *Lorna Doone* while Karen washed her hair and played her latest album and read a romance in between dancing energetically to the music.

Finally Arminel showered and took a sleeping pill and went to bed exhausted as if she had spent the day running. As she had, in a way—running from memories, running from herself, but most of all running from the implications of Kyle's presence.

They had decided to start early before the heat of the day and it was a wildly excited Felice who was first to hear the sounds of the horses' arrival on the crushed coral road.

'Oh, come *on*,' she begged for at least the twentieth time. 'Mummy, Karen, come on! You'll be late!'

Arminel laughed, fixed the hard hat firmly on to the curly head and said, 'No, darling, never with you around.'

Because Helen had insisted on providing the food they had only to take a bag of clothes and such necessities as the tropics make essential, as well as extra water for Felice, who dehydrated quickly.

Outside under the feathery shade of the palms the horses stood quietly, turning their curious heads towards the house as Felice ran down the path.

'Super morning,' Helen greeted them, her curious glance flickering from Kyle to Arminel and back to Kyle as he lifted Felice up on to the small pony which was hers.

'Lovely!' Arminel would never be as good a rider as Helen, or as Felice promised to be, but she had come a long way since Kyle had first put her up on to Tessa.

Now she smiled at the Fijian man who helped her into the saddle and asked him about his wife, who had just gladdened his heart by producing a delectable son.

After a few moments of organising they were ready to go. With them was the oldest of Helen and Tim's sons, a pleasant child named Martin who, at the age of eight, felt superior enough to Felice to keep an eye on her. The Shakespearean actor was also a member of the party. He viewed his mount with charming ruefulness and told a long but extremely funny story of the trials of coping with a horse in full armour in an epic film he had made in Spain.

It was delicious to ride through the plantation, the horses' hooves muffled on the soft grass, while about them birds and butterflies flew, as gaily coloured as the living jewels of the reef. Occasionally there came the faint smell of drying copra, the only indication apart from the trim rows of palms that much of the island was a working and profitable concern.

Once out of the plantation the original vegetation of the island clothed the rising ground and the soil changed from the sandy loam coconuts love to a rich volcanic red, freely interspersed with rocks ejected during one of the many volcanic explosions which had formed the Fijian islands aeons ago. Here grew bananas and the ubiquitous breadfruit with its great, immensely valuable fruit; the swampy patches held cultivated taro.

Then the ground became even steeper and the semi-cultivated air of the lower reaches vanished. The track wound through rain-forest seething with life, thick, almost oppressive in spite of the exquisite beauty of form and hue manifested in the dim depths beneath the canopy.

'Green,' Felice said cheerfully. 'All colours of green. Mummy, how long till we get to the top?'

'Quite a way yet, my cherub. Are you tired?'

A faintly disgusted look was her only answer. Felice had no intention of giving in even if she had to be strapped to her pony. A faint frown pulled at Arminel's brows. Sometimes it didn't seem normal for a child to be as determined as Felice.

'What's the matter?'

Kyle had dropped back and was looking at her with cool interrogation.

'Nothing.'

He wasn't fooled, of course. As his glance moved across to the child he said, 'She's managing very well. In fact, I'd say of the two of you she has more stamina. You look as though a flick of the finger would have you out for the count.'

If I treat him as just any man, she thought, just as if he were some nice man I've met for the first time, then maybe I can reach some sort of equilibrium. So she smiled without any hidden bitterness.

'As that sort of comment can usually be construed to mean that I look dreadful, I'll ignore it. How do you like our island?'

If her straightforward response surprised him no hint of it escaped. 'Very much. A perfect hideaway for the very rich. No stresses, no strains, surroundings of exquisite beauty and enough activity to fill the days so that one doesn't ever get bored.'

'Well, that's a backhanded compliment, if ever there was one,' she said cheerfully. 'Don't you approve of wealth, Kyle? Or is it your own kind you resent—and look down on?'

The broad shoulders moved in a shrug, but beneath his half-closed eyes his glance was shrewd and as sharp as a lance. 'I think you've read me wrongly. As you pointed out, I'm the last person to disapprove of wealth—if it's honestly gained.'

'You mean inherited?'

Damn, damn, damn, she hadn't intended to say that. It was offering open provocation!

He smiled narrowly, his eyes fixed for a moment on the gold gleam of her wedding ring. 'That doesn't worry me. If the inheritors are not fit to have it they usually dissipate it, give someone stronger and more able the chance to acquire it. What I dislike is the pursuit of wealth—or power—for its own sake. And the bartering of all self-respect for the things that money can buy.'

Oh, he knew how to hurt, each word exquisitely calculated to wound like an arrow, leaving behind poison that would fester for years.

Harking back to her earlier decision to forget the past and all that had happened, Arminel said lightly, 'Oh, I'm sure everyone dislikes that sort of person. But they usually make their own punishment, surely? A person lacking in self-respect is a poor apology for a human being.'

'How right you are,' he mocked.

It was all Arminel could do not to hit him across his handsome smiling face. *Anything* to wipe that taunting sneer from it. Even as her hands clenched she forced them to relax and repressed the turbulence of her emotions. Later, in the privacy of her own home, she could swear, or weep, or scream. While Kyle stayed on the island the only way to get through the days was to ignore him. And if it had the effect of maddening him, so much the better, some unregenerate part of her brain whispered.

So she composed her expression into one of smiling yet reserved interest. He is a pleasant stranger, she reminded herself. Aloud she asked, 'How long are you planning to stay?'

It was abrupt, but she had to know. And that would be the last betrayal. From now on in she would be Dan Evans' wife. And he could like it or loathe it, there was nothing he could do about it.

'Oh, for as long as Helen will have me,' he answered casually.

Hearing her name, Helen demanded to know why they were discussing her; after being told of his remark she said, 'Why, Kyle darling, you can stay as long as you like, you know that! Your mother said in her last letter that you haven't had a decent holiday for *years*! This is such a perfect place to unwind.'

'Oh, it is indeed,' he said, his expression coldly amused. 'Marvellous. Like a dream come true. If I'd planned it I'd never have found a better opportunity.'

Helen looked pleased, but to Arminel his words were ominously close to a threat. With wild frightened eyes she stared ahead until her lashes came down to hide her fear. Every instinct urged her to run, to get out of Fiji before he carried out whatever it was he had planned for her.

Only for a moment, and she was immediately ashamed of such a display of panic. Who was he to frighten her away? If he did it once he could do it again and again, finding out from Helen when she was holidaying there and reappearing each time like the ghost at the banquet.

After all, what could he do? Nothing. If she refused to allow him to see how much his poisoned remarks hurt he would never know, never realise that after all these years she was as hopelessly in love with him as she had been.

When she had married Dan she had started grimly on a programme of self-improvement, somewhat to his amusement, although he had encouraged it. Perhaps he had realised how inferior she had felt at Te Nawe when they had discussed books she had never heard of, people who were only names.

At first it had been a hard grind, but gradually she became enthusiastic, the beauty of the things she read engraving themselves on her brain, enriching her life.

Especially poetry, which for her had been almost destroyed at school by an insensitive teacher. When she was free to enjoy without having to analyse she found much unbearably beautiful and began to learn it.

Some lines came into her head now; when first she had read Sir Walter Raleigh's 'Walsinghame' she had hoped fervently that they were false. Now, it seemed, they were only too prophetic:

> 'But true love is a durable fire
> In the mind ever burning;
> Never sick, never old, never dead,
> From itself never turning.'

That was like her love. A durable fire, sometimes damped down, for long years dimly glowing coals, but always there, always burning beneath the prosaic surface of everyday life. If she gave into it, as she had once done, it could set her alight and burn her into ashes.

With a new resolution she looked around her, chin lifted delicately.

'You look as though you've come to some decision,' Kyle murmured, softly enough so that no one else heard him.

Willing her eyes to be frank and clear, she laughed. 'No, just remembering some poetry.'

One dark brow climbed. 'Do you make a habit of recalling poetry?'

'Frequently,' Karen chimed in, her voice dry. 'She learns the stuff, too.'

'A romantic, Arminel?'

She flashed him a smile, ignoring the sardonic inflection in the deep tones. 'Why not? It's fashionable once more to be romantic, didn't you know?'

Helen came in cheerfully, 'Kyle darling, all women are romantic; we'd all sacrifice our souls for the sort of love that poets praise and writers try to describe. It's only when we can't get it that we settle for husbands.'

Even Tim laughed at this, comfortably secure in the fact that although his wife could not help herself flirting with any handsome man he was one of the kingpins of her life.

The conversation became general, then petered out as the track wound its way across a steep pinch before reaching a kind of plateau. The sound of water falling from a height became louder. When they reached a cliff of blackish stone heavily overhung with creepers and ferns and orchids, green, primeval in its lushness, it was like cool music in their ears. A little stream chattered down from above before falling over the lip into a wide, smooth basin at which everyone looked yearningly. So far above sea-level the air was cooler, but cooler in the tropics was still hot, as Tim said, and he was not the only one whose shirt stuck to his back.

'Shall we swim now or on the way back?'

'Why not both ways?' Garth, the actor, was the hottest of them all. 'Speaking as a poor refugee from the northern hemisphere, I'm not sure that I can remain unmelted if there's much farther to go.'

Felice's demand for a drink decided them. 'My pony is hot, too,' she said pathetically. 'Can I give him a drink?'

'We'll do that first, shall we?' Kyle's tone made it quite clear that as far as he was concerned the horses always came first.

Arminel wondered if she was the only one who felt rebuked, but as she followed him down he was explaining to Felice that she was not to allow her mount to drink too deeply.

'Why?'

'Because horses have funny stomachs. If they get too hot and then drink a lot they get a terrible pain in their bellies. It's called colic and it hurts them very much.'

He would make a good father, she mused, then hastily banished the thought. It was too painful. Too stimulating, too.

Ten minutes later they were all swimming in the cool water. Felice crowing with laughter as she was given a vigorous ride on their Fijian guide's shoulders. As they frolicked Arminel lay quietly on her back, staring at the sky. In spite of a particularly bloodthirsty heritage the Fijians were the kindest, most charming people she had ever known, gentle, laughing giants with their magnificently strong faces and mops of bushy hair and their profound love for children, their own and everyone else's.

And their homeland must be one of the most beautiful spots in the world. Or three hundred of the most beautiful spots, for there are over three hundred islands—or five hundred depending on how big an island is considered to be—and of these a hundred are occupied.

Yet as she lay in the midst of jungle beneath a blazing tropical sky she remembered other hills, high and steep and grass-covered, sweeping down to a sea which was sometimes grey and turbulent, sometimes rivalled the turquoise waters about the island. And she knew a pang of homesickness that made her turn over on to her face in case anyone should surprise that anguish in her expression. Would she never forget it, the ecstasy of the skylarks above the paddocks, sheep bleating as they were crowded towards a gate by barking, fussing dogs, the uncompromising hard lines of the land.

The uncompromising, hard man who owned it and loved it and worked for it.

She swam, arms working fiercely, until someone stopped her and said something, laughing at the collision.

'Sorry, Garth,' she apologised, pushing her wet hair back from her face as she stood up.

'Oh, my pleasure. It's not often that such a beautiful woman sets off after me with complete determination.'

She laughed, wrinkling her nose at him. 'Then I won't tell you that I didn't even know that you were there.'

'No, don't do that,' he said comfortably. 'Do you think we'd better follow the others out, or shall we let them go on without us and make ourselves our own idyll here?'

'Better go, I suppose.' Because Kyle was watching

them she made it sound lightly regretful, a little flirtatious, but certainly not enough to be considered a come-on.

As she walked up on to the bank the water streamed from her in a silver sheet, from the wide golden shoulders to the curving provocative line of hips and thighs. She shook her head and ran her fingers through her hair, secure in the knowledge that beneath her swimsuit her body was as firm as a young girl's, glowing with health and vigour.

Kyle tossed her a towel, the line of his jaw particularly pronounced.

The rest of the trip was through more rain-forest, interspersed with moments of sheer beauty and some mild panic, as when Tai made them listen to a distant crashing and said succinctly, 'Pigs.'

'I've always intended to have a go at one,' said Tim. 'How good are you at pig-hunting, Kyle?'

The broad shoulders lifted. 'I used to go after them when I was young and foolish.'

'Well, let's see what we can organise. Like to have a go, Garth?'

'I'm always ready for a new experience. How exactly would we go about dispatching the beast?'

'Kill it with a knife,' Tai told him, and grinned at his expression. 'Take the dogs and follow them on foot. Before sunrise.'

Garth joined in the laugh at his expense with good humour and a spoken determination not to back down.

'But what do we do with it once we've caught our pig?' he asked.

'Well, we usually give it to the villagers and they make us a *meke*,' Arminel told him. 'A party with the food cooked in a *lovo*. That's an earth oven.' She looked at Felice, who was already smiling in anticipation. 'Felice eats so much that you'd think she was a little pig herself!'

'You eat a lot too,' Felice defended herself with her

usual determination. 'Last time you said you'd put on some weight and you had black coffee for *three days*!'

She was exaggerating, her mobile face asking that they join in her joke, which they did. Arminel grinned at her, her eyes very soft and warm as they rested on the flushed little face. Felice returned her look, her love and dependence written in her expression.

Oh, I love you, Arminel thought. I love you so.

And she knew she could never regret that bitter-sweet marriage to Dan.

At the top, where there was a cleared grassy space that looked out over the forested cliffs below and the slower slopes they had just climbed, Arminel caught her daughter's hand in hers and squeezed it.

It was the kind of scene to give rise to daydreams of the South Pacific, the sea so intensely hued that it robbed the sky of colour, yet in the blue there was a tapestry of other shades, jade and amethyst and emerald, a jewelled, glittering panorama scattered with other jewels, islands like their own. To the south was the large bulk of Fiji's main island, Viti Levu; by turning around they could see the second largest, Vanua Levu. And there were so many others; Tai pointed them out, gave their names and told them the old legend which explained why no swimmer in Fijian water need fear shark attacks.

'But you have to wear shoes on the reef,' Felice said importantly, her face dwarfed by the binoculars she was holding to her eyes.

'Can she actually see through them?' Helen asked beneath her breath.

'I don't think so.' Arminel laughed softly. 'But she likes to pretend.'

Helen smiled, looking complacently at her Martin, who was busy insisting that he could see a canoe about a hundred miles away.

Arminel turned, met the cold irony of Kyle's glance and remembered with a shock another occasion when she had stood on a hill and looked out over a land as beautiful as this, a sea as wide. Te Nawe was higher, but there had been the same sensation of being on top of the world. Only this was a drowsy, sensuous world, and that other had been exhilarating, crisp and stimulating.

For a long moment they looked at each other, then Kyle smiled, a cold, contemptuous movement of his lips.

I will not let him destroy my pleasure, she thought defiantly, but will power was no defence against his hard antagonism and in spite of her determination much of the shining delight of the day had gone.

In a way she was glad when at last they arrived back at the house. Felice had had to give in to her tiredness in the more taxing downhill stint and she had finished the trip up before Kyle, obviously enjoying herself immensely. Fiercely repressing jealousy—oh, to be jealous of her own child!—Arminel was glad when their little cavalcade came to a stop.

And when Felice was bade to thank Kyle she lifted her face and gave him an enthusiastic kiss, arms clinging tightly until he separated them with a disarming gentleness to hand her down to Arminel. His expression was remote, almost as though he was startled at his own reaction.

# CHAPTER NINE

At least the activities of the day summoned instant sleep. Unfortunately it was not enough to keep Arminel unconscious all night. She woke in the early hours and after a drink of water and half an hour's reading was forced to admit that she wasn't going to back to sleep.

If she lay here she would spend the time in totally unproductive and fruitless yearning.

A glance at the clock revealed that she had another three hours until dawn. Three hours spent longing hopelessly for a man she could never have was too much.

With sudden determination she got out of bed, tied the long deep rectangle of cotton that made a *sulu* above her breasts and slid her feet into leather thongs.

Outside it was quiet and still, the only sound the roar of the waves on the reef. No breeze separated the feathery fronds of the palms. The air was warm and dry, like a caress on her skin. In the sky an old moon gave enough light to make it easy to see where she was going. Through the darkness the greenish-yellow ylang-ylang flowers glimmered, powerfully scented. Sometimes it seemed that the whole island was bathed in that erotic perfume, for the Fijians scented coconut oil with it and used it to protect their skins from the sun. Arminel picked a flower and walked on down towards the beach. After a moment she made a motion to throw it away; the scent teased her nostrils unbearably, setting fire to numerous nerve-endings.

She knew what she wanted, of course. It was not the first time this intolerable restlessness had haunted her, driving her to excesses of work so that she could find

sleep and with it oblivion from the urgent needs of her
body. Five years ago Kyle had shown her just how
responsive she was, awakening needs and desires which
had never died. Mostly her sexuality slumbered,
sublimated by her enthusiasm for her studies, her busy
daily life, but on occasions it awoke and she was
miserably forced to admit that she craved for him.
Several times she had thought quite seriously of taking
a lover, but it had been forcibly made clear to her that
when she kissed it was Kyle she kissed, Kyle she
wanted, Kyle her body needed.

To all intents and purposes she was fixated on him,
and there was no way she was going to cold-bloodedly
make love to another man so that she could close her
eyes and pretend that he was Kyle.

Usually vigorous exercise helped; she had even used
the classic cold shower to good effect. But tonight he
was not twelve hundred miles from her, he lay sleeping
only a few score yards away. Her stomach tightened as
she thought of him sprawled across a bed, just as it had
clenched whenever her eyes rested on him during the
long, unbearable day.

'I love you,' she whispered, afraid even here of being
overheard. Clutched in her hand was the blossom she
had been going to throw away. 'Oh, what the hell,' she
said aloud, and reached down to tuck it between her
breasts.

The heavy sensuous perfume clung to her fingers.
With a swift motion she rubbed her hand down the side
of her *sulu* before setting off along the soft, heavy sand
of the beach. After a few minutes she stooped and took
off her thongs, dangling them from a forefinger.

Half way along the beach a rock made a convenient
marker; it had a flat top and was easy to climb, and
once she got up there she decided to stay, sitting with
her chin on her upraised knees, hands clasping her
ankles as she stared out across the bay.

The reef was a thin line of ghostly paleness against

the dark sea. Very faintly she could hear a distant noise; her eyes searched the skies until she picked up the big jet, its lights a garish intrusion in the night sky. Half-past three, she thought. Poor travellers! Even poorer staff at Nandi Airport!

'En route to Hawaii,' Kyle's voice said from behind her, and she gave a choked little cry and scrambled to her feet, her skin cold with shock.

'Frighten you, darling?' he asked unpleasantly. 'No, don't run away. You looked lonely sitting on your rock. Were you emulating a mermaid, waiting for some gullible sailor to come along?'

'If I was it seems I got one,' she returned in a shaky voice, hardly aware of what she said.

He smiled. 'Oh, not gullible. Never gullible, Arminel. Not even when I first knew you, before I really understood just how treacherous a woman could be.'

'Why did you dislike me so?' she asked, accepting the hand he held out. It was strong and warm, and when she was down on the sand again he refused to let her go as they walked slowly back along the beach. As if they were lovers, she thought achingly.

'I've told you.'

'No.' She shook her head. 'I can understand your mother's dislike. She already had Davina picked out for Rhys and after I'd been there a few days she must have realised that I wasn't the right one for him. Even if I'd had the right background, which you all made clear to me I hadn't.'

'You were a fish out of water, and you knew it.'

'None of you gave me credit for being a quick learner,' she snapped.

'No, although the fact that your husband could make—or break—most men probably helped no end in your acceptance in the world he inhabited,' he returned with smooth callousness.

Arminel shrugged off the hurt. Originally that might have been so, but she had made good friends since then

and she was no longer the under-educated gauche girl
who had thought that love could conquer all.

'Why were *you* so set against me?' she persisted. 'I
know you thought I was after Rhys's money, but I
refuse to believe that every girl who fell for him was
only interested in his bank balance. You weren't even
prepared to give me the benefit of the doubt, were you?
One look at me and you loathed me. Purely to satisfy
my curiosity, I'd like to know why.'

'Most of that glossy sophistication you wear is only a
veneer, isn't it?' He hesitated before continuing on a
strong note of self-mockery. 'One look was all it took,
Arminel. One look and I wanted you. I'm sure that I
don't need to tell you that an accident of birth gave you
a rare, thoroughly disturbing beauty. My heart sank
when I saw you come towards me. I thought, Oh God,
here's trouble, and trouble you certainly were.'

'And do you normally loathe and despise any woman
who attracts you?' she asked with an entirely spurious
air of interest. 'Is that why you're not married?'

His laughter angered her. She stiffened, jerking her
hand to free it, but as if he had expected such a reaction
his fingers tightened cruelly until she made a soft,
muffled sound. Then he said blandly,

'I like holding hands with you, darling. And I wasn't
just attracted to you, or by you. I lusted after you. My
brother was in love with you, or thought he was, and it
took me exactly five seconds to realise two things.'

'Which were?'

'That you weren't in love with him. And that whatever
leapt into life when I first looked at you was mutual. We
both knew it, and knew it for what it was. I learned to hate
you because you wouldn't let Rhys off that silken leash
you'd spun for him until you were sure of me. But I wasn't
so much at the mercy of my passions as you hoped, so you
had to play us both against each other, didn't you?'

'*No!*' she choked, appalled. 'Kyle, that's not—how
*could* you believe that of me?'

He pulled her to a stop, turning her with a quick painful movement, his hands on either side of her head holding it still so that he could look down into her face.

'What else could I believe?' he demanded harshly. 'Why didn't you tell Rhys immediately that you didn't want him?'

'Because he asked me not to. He wanted us to pretend. He felt he was being forced into a direction he didn't want to go.' She closed her eyes at the disbelief in his, then opened them again, desperate to convince him. The faint light emphasised the autocratic cast of his features, the hard, sensual line of his mouth and the pale fire of his eyes.

'You knew,' he said coldly. 'You flinched every time I came near you, you gave yourself away whenever I touched you. I tried you out in a hundred different ways and found you wanting. And all the time you kept Rhys dangling in case you didn't get me as far as the promise of a wedding ring.' He smiled as his hands tightened around her face. 'Did you really think I was fooled, darling? I'd been chased before, you know. Plenty of women like you want a man to take care of them all their lives so much that they're prepared to fall in love with his bank balance.'

'Oh, you fool!' Her voice throbbed with pain. 'Do you really believe that was all I wanted?'

'No, darling, the fact that you wanted me was a nice little piece of icing on a big, expensive cake, wasn't it? Tell me, did you want your husband as much?'

Whenever he said the words 'your husband' he made them an insult, and she reacted with passion and anger.

'I find you ugly,' she cried, her voice shaking. 'Ugly and prejudiced and hateful! Dan was ten times better than you could ever be!'

'Richer too,' Kyle agreed, then his hands slid to the nape of her neck and his head blocked out the light.

Her first mistake was trying to fight him. It took him no time to use his great strength to subdue her, his hands cruel as they held her still so that his mouth could take pleasure in hers. Then she stood motionless, fighting herself, so angry that the sudden uprush of desire took her by surprise. She went up like dry tinder, opening her mouth under his as she swayed towards him, her hands sliding up his arms to clasp his shoulders.

He lifted up his head and kissed her eyes closed, his hand tracing the line of her spine through the thin cotton *sulu*, discovering that beneath it she wore nothing. He whispered something and his hands on her hips pulled her close in to him and he was as aroused as she, the kiss they were exchanging was one of possession for both of them.

He is mine, she thought, amazed and afraid, and he knows it, and that, *that* is why he hates me. And the knowledge was so astonishing that she made no further pretence of resisting him as the rapture he made for her shook the stars.

Even as her body trembled, melted, became suffused with an aching, driving need, she knew she could not permit this. Last time Kyle had hated her, and things were no different now. Trapped in a relationship like flies in amber, they belonged to each other, but his bitter resentment lay between them, a gulf too wide to ford.

Slowly, because she didn't want to arouse his predatory instincts by her resistance, she pulled free, ignoring the sweet torment of his hands on her skin. Surprisingly he let her, only the harsh breathing revealing the depth of his desire. Beneath his brows the colourless glitter of his eyes burned, watching as she pulled the *sulu* tight about her, tucking it in. Her mouth throbbed, her body reproached her with a witless frustration, but she called on her reserves of will-power and pride.

'Sorry,' she said at last, looking at him.

'Why not?'

After a moment's hesitation she gave him the truth.

'Like most people I'm not particularly well equipped to deal with rejection. You may have forgotten how you behaved the last time I offered myself to you. I haven't.'

His anger was a tangible thing, but like her, he made some effort to control it. 'And if I said I have no intention of rejecting you?'

'Never?' she asked with a wise, wry smile. At the quick shake of his head she elaborated, 'Are you proposing, Kyle?'

His mouth pulled back to reveal his teeth. 'Marriage? I wouldn't marry you——' then he fell silent at her twisted smile.

'No,' she said even more wryly. 'I know. Well, believe it or not, Kyle, and I don't care much either way, I'm not in the market for a quick affair—or even a long-distance affair. Five years has given me a little more self-control—and sharpened my instincts of self-preservation. You did your best to break me once; it's not going to happen again.'

'You think not?' He didn't touch her, but his voice, deeply sensual, reached out and caressed her. 'And if I told you that breaking you is the last thing I want to do? What then?'

'Why,' she said, 'I shouldn't believe you, Kyle.'

All the way along the beach she felt the impact of his gaze, so tangible that the hairs on the back of her neck lifted as though she was in great danger.

As she probably was. Both of them knew that the boundary between acceptance and rejection was a very narrow, easily straddled one. If he had made love to her a little longer she might have objected but she would not have been able to hold out against the wild fever in her blood.

The reverse was also true, which made her wonder why he had let her go. She had felt the urgency of his desire, his blind need to lose himself in the silken sheath of her body, yet he had accepted her refusal.

When after a restless few hours she woke the next morning she knew why. Kyle wanted her willing, lost and subjugated so that his mastery was complete. And she lay for long minutes with her face pressed into the pillow while she moaned at the fate that had organised this unbearable coincidence.

However, her days of running were over. Never again was she going to turn her back on any situation because she thought she couldn't bear it. Living with Dan, watching his gallant fight against the inevitable deterioration of his body, had taught her that each person possesses the strength to face the worst life can throw their way.

She would not give Kyle the pleasure of knowing that she was defeated by the almost intolerable demands of her hungry heart. He knew, of course, how she was torn between her need of him and her self-respect; she could see an identical struggle taking place in him. The mere sight of him, his big, well-balanced body, the cutting line of his profile, the smooth bronze gleam of his proud head, was beautiful and dangerous to her. When his eyes rested broodingly on her, deep within their pale depths was a savage, self-derisory craving.

It was impossible to avoid him. As the hot, peaceful days drifted drowsily by they met all the time, down on the beach, riding, snorkelling; Helen gave a tennis party and Arminel ended up playing in a mixed doubles against Kyle and one of the McLauchlan girls, and being soundly trounced.

'Sorry,' said her partner cheerfully as he wiped his dripping brow on his sleeve. 'Hell, it's hot, isn't it! What on earth are we doing exhausting ourselves like this?'

'We're mad,' she agreed, trying to smile as she felt Kyle's hand close around hers in the traditional handshake. She made no effort to avoid his gaze, although a spark gleamed in hers at the mocking smile he gave. He had enjoyed beating her; well, if it appeased his ego, why not? she thought, and her mouth quirked.

Retribution was swift. As they walked off the court he dropped an arm about her shoulders, letting it lie heavily and possessively. If she tried to wriggle free he would keep her there, by force if necessary. She could feel the purpose emanating from him and tried her best to look as though it was merely a casual gesture. She might have carried it off, too, in spite of the inordinately interested glances from everyone else, if he hadn't pulled her head back and dropped a kiss on her brow.

Her eyes glared up at him, baffled and angry, as he said loudly enough to make sure everyone heard it, 'Never mind, darling. Better luck next time.'

'Better partner,' her partner said generously, helping himself to a long glass of something which tinkled with ice. 'Arminel deserves to play with someone like you, Kyle.'

'So I've been trying to convince her,' Kyle returned outrageously, and only Arminel could read the cold amusement in his eyes.

Thank heavens for children! Felice, totally ignoring the stunned silence that followed, positioned herself in front of him and said sturdily, 'I want a cuddle, too,' which got a general laugh and more or less forced Kyle to pick her up. But Felice wasn't satisfied with that. 'Mummy too,' she said imperiously, and to Arminel's horror Kyle pulled her close and the three of them were held together by her daughter's strong brown arms.

'Very touching,' Helen observed thoughtfully when Arminel had managed to break the clinch without too much fuss. 'You know, Arminel, you should be thinking about a father for her. Children need fathers.'

'Possibly.' The asperity in Arminel's voice was not hidden. 'But I don't need a husband.'

Helen looked pensive. 'You do, really. All women do. Oh, I know you pad out your time with your university things and good works, but it's all just a fill-in, isn't it?'

How to explain to her that although the charity work

was an obligation the papers Arminel was doing at university were exciting and stimulating? Helen had been brought up with only one aim in life, to marry well and be a good wife, and she was happy and contented in fulfilling that destiny. Feminism she viewed not so much with opposition as with a total lack of comprehension. A busy social life, her three sons, her husband, possibly in that order, filled her days so that she asked for nothing more.

It would be useless to try and convince her that Arminel's social life was a duty, most of it connected with the charities she supported. Except for a few close friends she held herself a little aloof from many who would gladly have befriended her. Dan had encouraged her to try for a degree, his confidence in her overcoming the diffidence she had felt. He had enjoyed being her mentor.

Now she said slowly, 'Not really. I'm not like you, Helen.'

'No,' Helen agreed.

Arminel hid a sad smile. She knew that Helen, like many people, wondered at her motives for marrying Dan. Those who knew her had come to realise, as Helen had, that the simplest explanation was not correct, but none of them knew the reason. Helen thought she was frigid, that all the warmth in her character was maternal, and she would probably be astounded and horrified if she knew just how wrong she was.

Back at home Karen asked shrewdly, 'Is Kyle trying to put the hard word on you?'

Arminel smiled, a masterpiece of irony. 'No, that was a little punishment.'

'You know each other really well, don't you?' Karen wrinkled her nose at Arminel's enquiring look. 'I'm not trying to be nosey—well, perhaps I am, but I know you, and you've changed since he appeared on the scene.'

'Oh, come on, now . . .'

'You needn't tell me anything if you don't want to, I'm not prying, but—well, if there's anything I can do.' Karen looked down at the length of her legs, brown and glistening with sunscreen. 'Since you came back from New Zealand you've hidden yourself behind a mask. It's been so long now that it's almost part of you, but I knew you before you put it on, and I've often wondered why it was necessary. Now I know. It was Kyle, wasn't it? He was the reason why it didn't work out with his brother.'

'Rhys.' Arminel turned her head away. 'Yes, he was the reason.'

'Well, what does he want now?'

'Whatever it is he's not getting it,' Arminel said flatly. 'What happened five years ago is dead amd buried and I'm not going to resurrect it.'

Karen snorted in disbelief. 'Oh, sure! Dead and buried, indeed! Whenever I get between you two I feel as though I'm being zapped with laser beams or rays of some sort! The air fairly hisses between you, yet you say you don't want to resurrect anything. Face facts, Arminel, it doesn't need resurrecting, it never died, it's just been hiding behind the door.'

Arminel shrugged. 'I can't help that.'

'Felice likes him, and you know it's not everyone she takes to. Why don't you give him a chance? He is,' she went on, 'the most exciting man I've ever met. Those eyes! And that smile, so knowledgeable, with a tiny hint of cruelty. You know, Arminel, he's the sort of man you trust implicitly.'

'Oh yes?'

Karen laughed at the dry cynicism of her friend's voice. 'No, not with women, though I'll bet he's totally trustworthy with someone else's woman. Why, what— oh!' She was silent, her brain working overtime as she stared at Arminel's suddenly white face. 'Oh,' she repeated. 'He was not, I gather. Yes, I see.'

Arminel met her gaze unflinchingly. Karen was not

an intellectual, but a sharp brain combined with a profound interest in humankind made her uncommonly far-sighted where people were concerned.

'Yes, I think I see,' she said now, and unexpectedly, 'Poor Arminel! And poor Kyle. People of immense integrity are very hard to handle when they breach that integrity. They don't forgive easily, not themselves and not the cause of their fall, either. They're a bit puritan in their consciences.'

'You're very quick,' Arminel said, her voice rather shaky.

'A pity,' Karen sighed. 'Because you and he would be good together. He has the kind of strength you need in a man and you wouldn't let him ride roughshod over you. A docile, clinging wife would bore him out of his skull, and you need someone who doesn't worship you for your looks and forget that there's a woman beneath them.'

Oh, Kyle had never forgotten the woman! But then he had never worshipped at the shrine of her beauty, either. The attraction between them had been instantaneous and volcanic, a conflagration which had finally overwhelmed them both, but it was more than solely physical. Somehow they matched each other. But their mutual attraction was doomed by that puritan conscience clever Karen had discerned. And by their stiffnecked pride. And by the fact that she was ruled by her fear of his inevitable rejection. She was not going to suffer again the aching desolation that had driven her into Dan's arms.

Better by far to refuse him.

'There's no future for us,' she said, her voice tight with determination. 'So let's leave it, shall we? By the way, isn't Sean Lambert rather interested?'

Karen's tan assumed a rosy hue. 'Sean Lambert,' she parried loftily, 'thinks he only has to whistle and any girl will come running.'

'Well! Seeing that he wangled an invitation especially to be here at the same time——'

'Oh, *don't*!' The younger woman jumped hastily to her feet, running her hands down the side of her dress as though her palms were suddenly sticky. 'He's got a nerve, chasing me all the way over here when he knows I—when I——'

'When he knows you're in love with him?'

Poor Karen's face crumpled. 'I'll get over it.'

'But why? And don't try telling me he doesn't return your feelings. He dotes, and you know it.'

'Yes, but it wouldn't work. His family wouldn't like it.'

Arminel lifted fine brows. 'Why?'

'A, because they're nicely rich and I've got nothing. B, because they're heavily into the social whirl and I'm an orphan, no background, no nothing. C, because he's a clever man and I'm just your average girl, earning my own living at a not too difficult job.'

Arminel sighed. 'I know how you feel,' she said sympathetically, 'but you're too selfconscious. His parents started off with nothing, you know. Every cent they've got they earned. The social whirl you're so frightened of is just their way of having fun. And they must be the least snobbish couple I know. Your background or lack of it means nothing, as you're well aware. As for Sean's brains—he doesn't want a university graduate, twit. He wants you, native cunning and kind heart and all.'

'He's so conceited!'

Arminel laughed, head flung back on to the cane chair, the rich warm sound lazy on the lazy air. 'So, take him down a peg or two, but don't try to fool me or yourself. He might be a little spoilt because he's good-looking and nice and things have always come easily to him, but he's not conceited.'

'You're awfully wise about other people's affairs,' Karen told her waspishly. 'Why don't you use some of that wisdom on yourself? The life you lead is not natural and you know it. It's just not normal to ignore men the way you do. You're a warm, loving, interesting human being, but you're afraid to come out from behind the prison bars you've made for yourself. What you need is someone who won't take no for an answer, someone you can't freeze off. Perhaps he might be able to help you rejoin the human race.'

'Any ideas as to who that might be?'

Karen swung around, her round pretty face dismayed at the question which had been posed in Kyle's most cynical voice.

'Oh, *hell!*' she muttered, carefully refraining from looking at Arminel's still, white countenance.

'Sorry.' But he didn't look in the least sorry. The pale glance searched smilingly over Karen's horrified expression as he said lightly, 'Don't look so appalled. I'm sure Arminel won't sack you for a bit of plain speaking.'

'Well, of course not.' Karen actually bristled, staring accusingly at him.

From somewhere Arminel found the strength to stand up. Hoping desperately that her composure was returning, she said with a cool lack of concern, 'Haven't you ever heard of knocking, Kyle? You could have been caught in some pretty nasty crossfire; Karen and I usually end up throwing things when we quarrel.'

A gleam of something like admiration glittered for a moment beneath the thick lashes as he swung towards her. 'I did try to raise someone, but you were too busy shouting to hear me. Shall I go out and try again?'

She laughed. 'No, don't be silly. Would you like a drink?'

'Something long and cold and non-alcoholic,' he said promptly, apparently content to take his cue from her.

As she poured him some of the fruit punch which Asena made up in gallons each morning she reaffirmed her decision to treat him with no more than the courtesy of a good and gracious hostess. And she would just have to hope that as she had made it clear that she didn't want an affair he would leave her alone.

No more jaunts in the moonlight, no more emotional confrontations, nothing more than the idle, well-bred common coinage of the social world, cool, polite conversation carefully calculated not to touch any emotion.

# CHAPTER TEN

KAREN thought she was mad, but loyally did her part, refusing to leave them alone, breaking up any conversation after a short time, behaving, in fact, like a good social secretary and an even better friend.

Of course Kyle was too astute not to realise what was happening. The third or so time that Karen and some man made a laughing foursome with them an ugly gleam in his eyes promised retribution, but he was no longer dealing with young, silly Arminel Lovett. Mrs Dan Evans was a different kettle of fish, poised, with an adroitness at avoiding embarrassing social situations which had been gained through five years. She flirted cheerfully and meaninglessly with Garth, who quoted Shakespeare at her and knew exactly what her attention was worth. Married and divorced twice, he was not looking for another wife, being far too enamoured of his freedom, but Arminel Evans was beautiful enough to stir anyone's blood and it flattered his ego to be the one she laughed with, even if she was, he decided, like so many exquisite women, basically in love with her looks and so frigid.

Arminel was quite happy with this reading of her character. He and Felice got on well enough together to make things pleasant, although, true to her stubborn character, Felice obstinately preferred Kyle and made it quite clear that this was so.

They sailed on the turquoise waters of the bay, water-skiied and introduced Garth to wind-surfing.

'It's just a knack,' Arminel told him as he viewed the wind-surfer with faint dismay. 'If you can sail you can do it. All you have to remember is that you steer by tilting the mast. You grab the boom and push it forward, it heads off the wind, pulled aft it goes into the wind.'

'Oh, that's all, is it?' said Garth, hands on hips as she showed him. 'O.K., dear heart, you demonstrate.'

Arminel loved wind-surfing. The thrill of gliding over the sea like a flying fish, the silence and freedom of it exhilarated her. So she grinned at him and pushed off, catching the wind almost immediately, legs braced as she concentrated on getting the utmost from the apparatus. Like a sea-bird she swooped across the still waters of the bay, capturing the essence of the wind and the sea. The sun beat down, dazzling even beneath the dark lenses she wore to protect her eyes, warming skin that was shining with sun-block and spray. Apart from the steady crashing of the waves on the reef it was quiet, although she could hear Felice's high-pitched squeals. For a moment her heart lifted; she almost felt as though life was worth living again.

Kyle's reappearance in her life had brought a lonely bitter ache which shadowed her days and the long restless nights. Misery ate into the fabric of her life so that she found herself longing for him to go away. Yet his presence filled her with a forbidden delight. Every time she saw him her heart jumped in her breast and she knew that if he did leave the island she would be desolate.

In effect, everything was exactly as it had been at Te Nawe. Near him she was tormented; if he went her world became an alien place and this time there would be no Dan to pick up the pieces.

So she was doing her best to re-erect a barrier between them, bricking her heart up behind the high walls of polite indifference and cool courtesy.

Walls which Kyle had every intention of sashing down. He made no secret of the fact that for him as well as her that physical magic still burned as brightly as ever; just as he'd made it perfectly clear that his basic opinion of her hadn't changed at all.

So—impasse. Frustration all round, she thought wearily as she brought the windsurfer back towards the beach. And, of course, there he was, big and lean and dominant beside Garth, watching. In the hot sun Arminel shivered, for he was always watching her, the pale cold eyes giving nothing away. In spite of Karen's help and her own avoidance she had begun to feel like prey stalked by some inexorable hunter, merciless, determined, swayed by no emotion but the lust to conquer.

On the beach Garth grinned cheerfully at her, curiosity only half hidden as his eyes moved from the cold pure lines of her face to Kyle's hard countenance.

'You make it look easy,' he said easily. 'Why not explain the basics to Kyle here? He's not done any either.'

'Oh, you just don't want to try,' She looked at him and then beyond, searching for Karen.

'She's gone back to your place.' Kyle's voice was coldly satisfied. 'Felice went with her.' So you're on your own, his tone said.

Arminel straightened. 'Well, if you want to have a go . . .'

'I do.'

He picked up the basics quickly; after a few minutes he took the wind-surfer out, balancing it perfectly against the wind, the lean athlete's body silhouetted against the brilliantly coloured sail.

'Some chap,' Garth observed, watching her.

'Yes.' The monosyllable lacked any expression.

'Why not put him out of his misery?'

She stiffened and he grinned without remorse. 'You can tell me to go to hell if you like, but it's a bit ridiculous, isn't it? He wants you and you want him, and neither of you will give an inch. I know it's not fashionable to say so at the moment, but when Kyle's character was forming Women's Lib was only in its infancy. He's not going to give in, so you'll have to. It's as simple as that.'

'Do you really think you're qualified to give an opinion?' she asked in a stifled voice, head averted.

'Why do you think I'm at the top of my tree, Arminel? Apart from the fact that I look good and I move well and my voice has been carefully trained, I'm a bloody good observer of human nature. Humanity in general, that's my hobby. I'm a people-watcher. Neither of you is simple, in fact you're both complex characters. I can see exactly why you've got yourselves into this situation. Pride can sometimes be stronger than love if you don't watch it.'

'Love?' She laughed bitterly. 'What makes you think love has anything to do with us?'

'Hasn't it? Why else is he bitterly jealous of anyone who flirts with you? Look, he's coming back in now. He doesn't like to see you and me alone for too long.'

'You might be a brilliant observer of human nature,' she said wryly, 'and you're an extremely nice man, but Kyle is one on his own. The normal—oh!'

For the wind-surfer spun and Kyle disappeared below the surface.

Garth laughed, but when no bobbing black head appeared above the surface he said uneasily, 'Surely he should——'

'There's coral all through there!' Arminel was already running down the soft, clinging sand towards the empty sea. Garth overtook her, diving through the water with all the strength and speed of his masculinity as he covered the fifty yards or so to where the wind-surfer bobbed like a butterfly with broken wings.

It wasn't deep, and the water was crystal clear. When, Arminel reached the spot Garth had already dived and was on his way up again, dragging an obviously unconscious Kyle with him.

'I can get him in,' he gasped. 'Get ashore!'

Arminel found that panic produced such a massive surge of adrenalin that she was back ashore without even realising it. Kyle was heavy, too heavy for Garth to do more than drag him free of the waves.

'On his back,' Arminel gasped, helping him to pull Kyle's flaccid body over. 'Is he——?'

She dropped on her knees, supported the nape of his neck and pushed his head backwards, lifting the strong chin upwards. The wide chest remained inert. Banishing her terror, she lowered her mouth to cover his and began to breathe, into it, pinching his nostrils together.

'Good girl,' said Garth, stooping to hold his fingers against the carotid pulse in the brown throat. 'His heart's still beating. He'll be all right. He couldn't have been under water for more than a minute—that's well within the safety margin.'

Three times Arminel's breath lifted Kyle's chest, three times she watched it fall, then he gave a gasp and his chest rose of its own accord. The dreadful pallor receded, he began to choke.

'Quick, turn him over.'

It took their combined efforts to get him into the recovery position, his head turned to one side as he lay halfway on to his stomach, his hand by his face. The wide shoulders heaved; he began to retch.

Arminel collapsed on to the yielding sand, paper-white and trembling, tears running down her face. Dimly she heard voices from farther up the beach. Garth pushed her head between her knees and the world swayed.

An hour later Kyle was on his way to the hospital in Suva and Arminel was shivering on her bed, her mouth dry with the taste of the brandy Karen had forced on her, her mind cowering from the images that filled it.

'Mummy?' Felice peeped around the door. 'Mummy, can I come in with you? Karen said you might like me.'

Wise, clever, darling Karen. With her daughter's sturdy little body warm against her that dreadful shivering eased and faded.

'Poor Kyle,' said Felice. 'What will he do in hospital, Mummy?'

'Rest. They'll look at his head to make sure that it's all right.'

'He banged it on the coral, didn't he? Is that where all the blood came from?'

'Yes, he grazed it badly.'

'That's why you wear sandshoes.' The little voice was important. 'Mummy, was he going to die?'

Pain clutched at Arminel's body. 'He might have, if Garth hadn't been there. He—he pulled him up.'

'And you made him breathe again.' The small body squirmed. 'I like Kyle. He's nice. I'm glad he's not going to die. He's nice . . .' she repeated, yawning.

As she lay on the big bed Arminel stared at the ceiling and listened to her child's quiet breathing; slowly, out of the hours of pain and relief, a resolution formed within her brain. You must be the one to give in, Garth had said, watching her with those knowing eyes. What he had meant was that Kyle would never surrender. Well, she had always known that. These days on the island she had been fighting her own instinct to give him that surrender he needed while trying to find some way to accept what he offered without losing her pride or self-respect.

Now she knew that self-respect did not depend on anyone's opinion of her but her own. Not even Kyle's, which left only pride.

And after seeing his limp body so close to death she knew pride no longer meant anything. If he had died— well, if he had died something in her would have died too, for he was inextricably part of her now.

Could she accept his desire and his disdain? Lie in his arms in the frantic sensuality only he could arouse and know that to him she was a woman who had sold herself for the good life?

It would be difficult, but she could do it. And after a while perhaps he would come to understand her better. Could she cope with the rejection she had always seen as inevitable? Yes, she was strong enough for that.

Perhaps there would be no need for that, though. If she gave him a child . . . Her whole being clenched, then relaxed. Yes, if she gave him a child he was possessive enough to want it to bear his name. It was the oldest ploy in the world, but there was an additional twist. She would not need to marry him. Oh, there would be gossip, some of it highly unpleasant, but she could outface that.

Money talks, she thought wryly. Dan's money. And if he ever asked her to marry him she could tell him of that condition in Dan's will which had so upset the lawyer. What it amounted to was a complete repudiation of her if she married again. Everything went to Felice. If Kyle asked her to marry him surely he would realise that she was giving up an enormous income for him. Kyle too was rich, richer by far than most men, but Dan had been a multi-millionaire.

Surely that would prove that she thought little of material assets? Beside her Felice sighed and turned away, her smooth face creased by its contact with the pillow. Arminel echoed her sigh. That was all in the lap of the gods. She could only make her throw and hope for the best. Those minutes on the beach this afternoon had shown her exactly what life without Kyle would be. Nothing could be worse than that. Nothing.

He came back the next day and ignored Helen's scandalised objections to walk down to the beach. It was late afternoon and the day was still hot; Karen and Felice were shelling out on the reef with Garth and Samuela, Asena's husband. Arminel had watched them for a time from the shade of the coconut palms, but when Kyle appeared she had got to her feet and was on her way back to the house.

The sight of his figure stopped her. She pressed back against a palm tree and watched him with a steady gaze as he came towards her, lean and purposeful, the sun gilding his bronze hair into flames.

'Hello,' she said conversationally. 'You look fine. How's the head?'

'Not even a headache.' The deep voice was cool, but he was watchful.

Arminel resisted the temptation to touch the red stain which showed where antiseptic had been painted on to the coral graze.

'It pays to have a hard head,' she said lightly, suddenly nervous.

He smiled. 'It does indeed.' For the first time he looked around. 'No Karen?' he drawled. 'Didn't you expect me back so soon?'

'I should have known better.'

'You should have indeed.' A pause before he said, 'I believe I have you to thank for saving my life.'

Embarrassed and wary, Arminel shrugged and turned towards the path, walking through a thicket of banana palms. The wide fringed leaves hung limply; beneath them the grass was coarse and green. High above the coconut palms swayed gently. It was a still, green haven and she was very conscious of the fact that there was not a soul in sight; even if someone came along either the path of the beach they could not be seen.

Something like panic quickened her steps. Over her shoulder she said, 'Don't be silly, Kyle. I don't need your thanks. If you want to give them to anyone then thank Garth. He got you up from the bottom and on to shore.'

His hand on her shoulder stopped her in mid-stride. 'I've already thanked Garth,' he bit out, turning her to face him. 'Why are you running away? Do I frighten you?'

'When have you not?'

The hard grey eyes scanned her face speculatively while she looked up at him in an agony of apprehension. His face tightened.

'You don't really mean that,' he said, icily unpleasant. 'I can think of several occasions when you forgot any fear you might have had. In fact, I often think of those occasions.'

Arminel stared at him then turned away, angry as only he could make her.

'Don't turn your back on me!' he gritted, long fingers closing with hurtful force over the smooth bone of her shoulder.

She looked back, the dark blue of her gaze cool and cynical. 'I turned my back on you five years ago,' she reminded him, grabbing for control. 'You watched me go, remember, and never said a word to stop me. I find your behaviour now rather strange.'

He was held in the grip of some powerful emotion; she could feel it against her skin, a dark force gathering to rend her, intent on hurting her. For a moment she was afraid until she thought of Dan, meeting death with dignity and courage. Her chin lifted as her eyes, maddeningly composed, met his.

'Every time I see you,' he said between his teeth, 'I see dollar signs.'

'And do you think it's any different for me?' Her face had whitened, but she held fast to her courage. 'You're obsessed with money!'

'No, I'm obsessed with you.'

She held his gaze, her own ironic and weary. 'Do you still blame me entirely, the temptress who seduced you in spite of yourself?'

For a moment she thought she had pushed him too far. His teeth snapped together and from deep in his throat came a harsh noise like an animal in great pain. And then he was dragging her back against him, the hand which had been free joining the other to bind her tightly to him as he bent his head and spoke into the curve where her neck met her shoulder.

'I remember everything,' he said thickly. 'I remember how you begged me not to take you—and later, how you pleaded with me to make love to you because you were burning up and couldn't bear it. Do you remember that, Arminel? Do you?' His lips moved against his skin, as dry and hot as if he had a fever. 'I've never forgotten. And I'm going to take you again because I must have it. I want it again and again because it's never been like that for me since. Whatever you did to me that night was permanent, it left a mark on my body, it changed my brain patterns. I've had women since then and each time I knew it was going to happen, their face would change and I'd be staring into your wild eyes as they drowned me in desire. And I'd hear your voice——'

Somehow she had been turned in his arms so that they were standing face to face, his hands cupping her face, trembling, his low, impassioned voice harsh with feeling, hurting her ears, although of course she knew that there must have been other women, he was a sensual man. Her jealousy thickened, clotted in her throat. To stop the bitter words she swung her hand across his mouth.

'Shut up!' she hissed, watching as the mark of her fingers reddened against the teak tan skin. 'How dare you! I could kill you . . .' Her hand moved slowly, lovingly over the mark of the blow, her fingers smoothing the sore skin, massaging it.

'How do you think I felt when I heard that you'd married?' Kyle drew a ragged breath, his smoky eyes hazed with pain and anger. '*I* wanted to kill *you*. I would have killed you if I'd seen you. You knew you were mine, didn't you? *Didn't you!*' shaking her as she closed her eyes.

'You threw me out. I begged with you to let me stay, I said I would be exactly what you wanted if you'd only let me stay near you, and you said I was . . .'

'No, no, my darling.' This time it was his hand, but it was gentle and beneath it her lips moved as she kissed it. 'Oh, God,' he groaned, 'you terrify me. Until I met you I'd always been the one in control, able to take what I wanted, detached. No woman had ever meant more to me than an attractive companion to amuse myself with. Then Rhys brought you back as if you were a jewel for his finger and all the devils in hell laughed at me. I only had to hear your voice and I felt my hunger claw at my guts; I loved Rhys, and at night all I could think of was of Rhys's girl in my arms, in my bed. And the hell of it was that I knew it was the same for you. And you would do nothing about it. Why? Why didn't you tell him it was over?'

She shuddered at the husky, dangerous note in his voice, the hurried angry words. Above his hard mouth tiny beads of sweat gleamed on his skin. It was always hot here, but this was a different heat, primeval, his desire summoning an answering desire from her, and between them tension sang and quivered.

'Kyle,' she whispered, 'I must—Kyle, we'd better go back to the house. Please!'

He watched the words form on her lips, the soft trembling movements, and said savagely, 'You drive me mad! With you I lose all self-control, and you like that, don't you? You hated the fact that loyalty to my brother could keep me from accepting the invitation you offered, and you tantalised me until I could bear it no longer. Then you left, but you were always there, wherever I went, tormenting me until——' He stopped, breathing deeply and erratically, the pupils of his eyes dilated as they registered her fear. 'No!' he groaned, as the proud head bent and he rested his forehead on her shoulder.

Very gently she touched his heated skin, her mouth moving in small kisses over his cheek and the hard angle of his jaw. The sun's rays diffused in golden streams through the canopy of leaves. A small butterfly became a miracle of glowing colour as it flew up towards the canopy. Kyle began to speak again, muttering in a thick monotone so that she had to strain to catch the words.

'I've tried so hard to hate your ghost,' he said wearily, 'blamed you for the fact that I wanted you, and all the time I knew it would come to this, me pleading for your love, unable to fight it any longer. No, don't say anything, not yet. Please just hold me.'

But she did more than that, offering, with a generosity which made him speechless, the matchless comfort of her body.

'See,' she said smiling at him as she slipped free from the maillot she wore, 'I can hold you so much better when you lie in my arms.'

This time he loved her with a desperation that was little short of savagery, reinforcing his ownership of her body with a hard thrusting desire which should have frightened and hurt her, but she found that, as before, her need flared to meet and match his, so that they came together in the hot green shade beneath the banana palms in a frenzy of passion that left them too exhausted to do anything but lie clasped together in the slow downward spiral of satiation.

At last Kyle lifted his head and touched his mouth to her throat and the delicate curve of her breast. 'I love you,' he said, almost without expression. 'What are we going to do about it?'

'What do you want to do about it?' Her fingers moved up the back of his head, revelling in the damp thickness of the hair.

'Stay here with you and make love to you for several years,' he said, 'but I suppose our separate and collective responsibilities will put paid to that scheme. Do you feel up to marrying me?'

'Do I feel up to heaven?' she returned dreamily. 'No, but when it's offered to me I'd be stupid not to take it. There is one thing, though, Kyle.'

He lifted his head and looked down into the perfect flushed face.

'And that is?'

'If I marry again I lose my income. All I get is enough to keep Felice. Dan left the money in trust for her.'

For a long moment he stayed silent, looking into her face with a cool watchfulness that chilled her heart. 'So?' he asked softly.

She touched his mouth with a fingertip, but it was unresponsive. 'Do you mind?'

'Should I?'

'Well, you won't be getting a rich widow for a wife,' she said deliberately, because it had to be said. 'I'll come to you with nothing.'

The smoky eyes had hardened to granite as she spoke, but her last few words made him close them as if he was in pain. 'Are you trying to pay me back for the insults I flung at you?' he asked raggedly. 'Do you think it matters to me whether you have any money or not? God knows, I'm not poor. And I'm afraid I'm a jealous man. If you brought jewellery that your—that had been bought for you by your first husband I would refuse to let you wear it. Save it for Felice. From now on you'll have only what I give you.'

'And Felice?'

He reacted to her whispered query with a twisted smile. 'Oh, I like her,' he said wryly. 'She has guts and style, like her mother. I couldn't hate a child, or be jealous of her. We understand each other, Felice and I.'

'Yes,' she said thankfully, and smiled a little ruefully. 'I've been jealous these last few days of my own daughter. It's a horrid sensation, believe you me.'

He grinned. 'Good, serves you right. That haughty touch-me-not air you wore was like a red cloak to a bull.' His head turned, he listened, then got to his feet, pulling her up with him. His arms slid behind her shoulders; he stood, staring down into her face with a kind of devouring thankfulness. 'It does't worry you at all, does it?' he said softly. 'You'll give up everything for me.'

'Everything but Felice,' Arminel said soberly, aware that, far-sighted as ever, Dan had planned for this contingency. That puzzling proviso in his will had been drafted to ensure that if she married again it would be for love, not his money. And in her happiness she spared a thought for him, hoping that wherever he was now he would be as happy as she was.

'I don't expect you to give her up,' said Kyle, releasing her to pick up the clothes they had discarded. 'Come on, you shameless wench, get dressed before someone sends out a search party for us. You may not give a fig for your reputation, but I do.'

She laughed, watching unashamedly as he pulled on his shorts, draped his shirt over his shoulder. Then, reluctantly, and taking some considerable time, because he insisted on helping her, she wriggled back into her bathing suit.

Much later that night, when an ecstatic Felice had been finally tucked up in bed, and Karen had rather coyly taken herself off, they sat on the wide terrace and watched the moon come up through the coconut palms and listened to a lovesick dove crooning its sweet monotonous call. Arminel lifted her head from Kyle's shoulder and asked carefully,

'How is your mother going to react to my arrival on the scene, darling?'

'She knows how I feel about you,' he astounded her by answering. 'She won't be particularly surprised.' He drew her back to him, his fingers gently smoothing the curve of her cheek and jaw. 'She only disliked you because she could see the potential for trouble you brought with you. She knew you were wrong for Rhys; after a few days she realised that I was attracted to you. She wasn't very happy about that, either. Being an astute woman she knew that I was in trouble, and it didn't warm her heart towards you.'

'Does she know . . .?'

'How can she? And if she guessed, why should she blame you? Had I been able to keep my hands off you nothing would have happened. It was my lack of self-control. That was why I was so cruel to you. I couldn't hide from my guilt. You may have forgotten, but when I came into your room that night you begged me to go away. I almost raped you.'

'The operative word being "almost",' she said drily.

'I seem to remember that you received considerable co-
operation before too much time had passed. If I'd had
any sense I'd have left Te Nawe as soon as I realised I
was falling in love with you, but I thought that because
you seemed to hate me I was quite safe. And it was such
a bitter pleasure to be in the same room as you that I
couldn't bear to go.'

'Oh, my lovely lady,' he groaned, pulling her across
to lie in his lap. 'Why do you think I didn't send you
away? You were a constant torment, one that I couldn't
do without. At night I would pace the floor, imagining
you closing those sleepy blue eyes in ecstasy as I made
love to you, and I would find myself savagely, bitterly
angry with Rhys, because you laughed with him and let
him touch you. I don't think I was sane after the first
minute I saw you. You looked at me with a kind of
shock, your eyes dilated, your lips trembling, and I felt
my whole body clench.'

They kissed, and kissed again, seeking and finding,
until the hot tide of desire threatened to overwhelm
them and Arminel broke the embrace, murmuring, 'No,
no, dearest. Not now. Not here.'

'Mm.' He groaned, his mouth travelling down the
smooth arc of her throat. 'I don't know that I want
such a sensible wife.'

She laughed softly, holding his head against her. The
skin of his face was hot, his open mouth erotically
disturbing, and she shuddered, feeling again the warmth
and hunger deep in the pit of her stomach. 'Sensible?'
she muttered into his hair. 'I don't feel at all sensible
now. But darling, we must be.'

'Yes, I know. When will you marry me?'

She looked into his eyes, smiled softly and said, 'I feel
married to you now.'

The grey eyes narrowed. Beneath his lashes she
could see leaping points of light as they swept her face,
lingering with mocking thoroughness on the slightly
swollen lips and glazed, dreamy gaze. 'Oh, do you?' said

Kyle as he slid his hand beneath her breast and turned it to cup the soft fullness. 'Just as well, my lady, because I feel very much married to you. But no more worrying, hmm? You'll find that my mother will accept you without any recriminations at all. You may not be exactly what or who she had in mind for a daughter-in-law, but she's known for a long time that her only hope of acquiring a wife for me was for me to find you again.'

He was probably right, and at the moment she didn't care all that much anyway. The way she felt now, she could deal with a hundred mothers-in-law and come off triumphant.

'Had you planned never to marry?' she asked in a soft, awed voice.

'Not if I couldn't have you. And I was quite sure I didn't want the sort of woman you'd shown yourself to be.'

'I suppose not. Money-hungry, greedy, shallow and pro——'

'Hush,' he said before he silenced her by the simple method of covering her mouth with his. A long time later, when the trembling in her limbs was made worse by the same trembling in his, he said with painful honesty, 'What else could I think? You'd appeared from nowhere engaged to my brother, but although you wanted me you wouldn't break it off with him. You tempted me and taunted me and drove me out of my mind, told me you loved me—and then only a month after you'd left me my mother was reading out the report of your marriage to a man who was old enough to be your father and a millionaire twenty times over. I hated you because you'd made a fool of me. Why did you marry him, Arminel?'

Quietly, holding him tenderly, she told him about that flight across the Tasman, and the mixture of compassion and exhaustion and desolation which had brought about that marriage. Her affection for Dan

was clear in her tones; not even for Kyle was she going
to conceal just how much he had meant to her, in spite
of that jealousy he had spoken of.

'He knew you better than I ever did,' he said when
she had finished, his voice harsh with self-condemna-
tion. 'Did he love you, Arminel?'

'Yes, my poor Dan.'

'And you?'

'I grew to become very fond of him.'

'Poor devil. And I thought I lived in hell! It must
have been refined torture for him to love you and know
that he had only your affection.'

Arminel could have wept for this evidence of his
compassion for the one man he had cause to resent.
One day she would tell him why Dan had made that
stipulation in his will about remarriage, but not now.

For the moment it was enough that in spite of his
jealousy there was enough compassion to make her first
marriage no longer a taboo subject. She would not have
to watch every word she said, or teach Felice about her
father in secret.

'Oh, I love you,' she whispered, pressing tiny fevered
kisses across the stark line of his cheekbone. 'I love you
so much that I'll never be able to show you. I worship
you, I adore you. . . .'

'Hush,' Kyle muttered, a smile creasing his cheek.
'Shameless creature! How do you think I feel about
you? As though all skies are dark without you, as
though you are all that I need to live, the breath in my
body, the blood in my veins, the other part of me. After
all these years of being incomplete I've found the one
person who makes life anything more than a weary
procession of days wearily endured. And to think that
when I saw you again I believed I hated you!'

'Ah, but that was because you still thought I was the
greedy unprincipled baggage who'd married for money.
How could you love anyone like that?'

Her voice was light; she had hoped to make him

laugh. Instead he lifted his hand and ran his finger across the slender width of her throat.

'No,' he said harshly. 'You still don't understand, do you? I hated you because I took one look at you, so exclusive, cool and poised, with all the advantages of the money you'd sold yourself for, and I knew I loved you, that whatever you were, whatever you did, you held my heart and soul in fee. I wanted to kill you for being so beautiful and so damned ugly inside, and I knew all the time that I was going to end up crawling across broken glass to get to you, because it was quite obvious that the old magic was still very much there. My emotions were a very explosive mixture—desire, bitterness and contempt, and all I felt for myself was a savage derision.' He drew a deep, jagged breath, the smoky eyes blazing into hers, his features thrown into harsh relief by the intensity of his emotions. 'You called me a barbarian. If you'd known how close you were to the mark you'd have turned tail and fled.'

'I came very close to it several times' she confessed, shaken to her soul by his bitter revelation, 'but I couldn't. I told myself that it was because I wasn't going to run again, that you had no right to drive me away from here too, but I was fooling myself. It was because no matter how you treated me, I was happier with you near me than apart.'

'Darling,' he whispered, pushing her back into the cushions, 'my sweet lady, my only love, how can you still love me after all that I've done to you?'

Her eyes teased, hiding the depths of emotion he had summoned. 'With difficulty,' she murmured, and then, as his mouth hovered a kiss's breadth away from hers. 'Oh, so easily, my love. I only had to ask myself what life would be like without you, and after I'd recovered from the panic that that thought produced, I knew.'

When she could breathe again she confessed, 'Yesterday, after the plane had left for Suva, I decided, quite coldbloodedly, that I was going to seduce you. All

my scruples, my pride, every sensible reason for having
nothing to do with you fled when I realised you could
have died. I decided I would have an affair with you in
the hope that you would realise just how much I did
love you.'

She didn't dare tell him about that other, even more
irresponsible decision to have his child. But he said quietly,
'And I would have taken you on any terms, once it
came to the crunch. Like you, I thought fairly seriously
while I lay in that hospital. Nothing seemed important
except that I could have died without ever holding you
again.' He bent his head, his avid mouth searching out
the contours of her breast beneath the fragile cotton
lace she was wearing. And when she sighed voluptuously
and wriggled down so that the hard length of his body
half overlaid hers, he added, 'Tell me, once you'd
seduced me, did you plan to give Felice a small brother
or sister?'

Arminel had never thought to blush again, but at his
words a scalding tide of colour washed up from her
throat and she turned her head into his chest, seeking to
avoid his laughing, mocking gaze. 'How well you know
me,' he murmured, strong fingers turning her chin to
his merciless scrutiny. 'Because I would never have let a
child of mine grow up not knowing its father. Had you
that in mind, too?'

Shamed, she nodded, and he laughed, and kissed her,
tormenting little kisses, holding her down with the
weight of his body as she struggled to get free.

'You, my lovely, are totally without scruples,' he said
severely, then spoilt the effect by adding deeply, 'I wish
I'd let you do it; I'd like to be seduced by you.'

Arminel kissed his chin, and then the pulse that beat
in his throat, and then the small patch of skin at the
base of the open neck of his shirt. 'On our wedding
night I shall seduce you in every way I know,' she
promised. 'I'm not particularly experienced, but I have
a vivid imagination. And love helps, doesn't it?'

Every muscle of the big body tensed. Kyle looked at her with such naked need that she made a soft little sound of despair, and then he relaxed and sat up, drew her up beside him and said quietly, 'I'll look forward to that, dear heart. We've plenty of time. All the time in the world, now.'

And Arminel smiled and agreed as hand in hand they went back into the house. She did not say it, but her whole being thanked her kindly, clever Dan who had so carefully left this path open to a happiness he had never known. Together there was nothing they could not do, she and Kyle. And Felice, and those other children who would be theirs to love and care for. But for the moment, this was enough.

# A WORD ABOUT THE AUTHOR

Robyn Donald cannot remember ever being unable to read. She learned the skill at a very early age; and today, she claims, reading remains one of her great pleasures, "if not a vice."

Robyn, her husband and their two children make their home in a small country village in the historic Bay of Islands in the far north of New Zealand. Both the climate and the people are friendly, and her family enjoys sailing in particular and the outdoor life in general.

Her other interests include cooking, music and astronomy. And she finds history and archaeology especially fascinating because "they are about the sum total of human experience."

When she writes, Robyn visualizes scenes that she knows and loves. The actual germ of a story arrives "ready-made from some recess of my brain, but," she adds, "it takes quite a while to work out the details!"

# Coming Next Month in Harlequin Presents!

**703 THE WALL   Amanda Carpenter**
A lonely Lake Michigan shore seems an unlikely place for a tormented reclusive writer to meet a beautiful singing star. But meet—and love—they do, in this passionate and sensitive romance.

**704 DARK PARADISE   Sara Craven**
For special reasons of her own, a young woman feigns interest in a crusading journalist and accompanies him to the West Indies—where events change her pretend love to the real thing!

**705 DANCE WHILE YOU CAN   Claire Harrison**
A dedicated dancer doesn't have room in her life for love *and* career. So thinks a lovely Manhattan prima ballerina—until a holiday affair with a handsome businessman wreaks havoc with her philosophy.

**706 SHADOW MARRIAGE   Penny Jordan**
Deep in their hearts, an estranged husband and wife, both a part of Hollywood's glamorous film industry, know they need to reconcile to find happiness...yet cruel Fate seems to have other plans.

**707 ILLUSION OF LOVE   Patricia Lake**
An intriguing tale of romance, jealousy and passion that sweeps from a beautiful South Pacific island to an English manor by the sea, and culminates on a luxurious yacht on the French Riviera.

**708 GOING UNDERGROUND   Karen van der Zee**
When a taxing career pushes her to the edge, a young woman spends two months in Virginia helping a handsome single parent with his son. In so doing she discovers her inner strength...and capacity for love.

**709 IMPRUDENT CHALLENGE   Jessica Steele**
A plucky English miss visits her suddenly bankrupt father in Japan to delve into the cause of his financial crisis—only to find herself falling for the very man responsible for it!

**710 THE INHERITANCE   Kay Thorpe**
When an English girl inherits a ranch in Florida, she travels there with the intention of selling...but when she meets, and dislikes on sight, the arrogant would-be buyer, she quickly changes her mind.

# Harlequin Photo Calendar

## Turn Your Favorite Photo into a Calendar.

JULY 1984

The Browns

Uniquely yours, this 10x17½" calendar features your favorite photograph, with any name you wish in attractive lettering at the bottom. A delightfully personal and practical idea!

Send us your favorite color print, black-and-white print, negative, or slide, any size (we'll return it), along with **3** proofs of purchase (coupon below) from a June or July release of Harlequin Romance, Harlequin Presents, Harlequin Superromance, Harlequin American Romance or Harlequin Temptation, plus $5.75 (includes shipping and handling).